Alessandro shook his head. "I've watched you for weeks, Little Mouse, trying to avoid me."

Her lips parted in shock. He'd noticed her?

"I have a reputation for breaking hearts, but the fact is I always tell women the truth, *cara*," he said, looking at her. "So let me be clear. Our romance tonight will be only an illusion. A means to an end for both of us. I will not call you tomorrow. I will not call you ever. You will return to being my employee. And I will be your boss, pretending not to notice as you scurry away in the shadows."

Lilley licked her lips, searching his gaze. "You mean if I go with you to the ball tonight you'll ignore me tomorrow? You'll ignore me forever?"

"That's exactly what I mean."

Jennie Lucas grew up dreaming about faraway lands. At fifteen, hungry for experience beyond the borders of her small Idaho city, she went to a Connecticut boarding school on scholarship. She took her first solo trip to Europe at sixteen, then put off college and travelled around the US, supporting herself with jobs as diverse as gas station cashier and newspaper advertising assistant.

At twenty-two she met the man who would be her husband. After their marriage she graduated from Kent State with a degree in English. Seven years after she started writing she got the magical call from London that turned her into a published author.

Since then life has been hectic, with a new writing career, a sexy husband and two small children, but she's having a wonderful (albeit sleepless) time. She loves immersing herself in dramatic, glamorous, passionate stories. Maybe she can't physically travel to Morocco or Spain right now, but for a few hours a day, while her children are sleeping, she can be there in her books.

Jennie loves to hear from her readers. You can visit her website at www.jennielucas.com, or drop her a note at jennie@jennielucas.com

Recent titles by the same author:

RECKLESS NIGHT IN RIO
THE VIRGIN'S CHOICE
SENSIBLE HOUSEKEEPER, SCANDALOUSLY PREGNANT

A NIGHT OF LIVING DANGEROUSLY

BY

JENNIE LUCAS

All the characters in this book have no existence outside the imagination of the author, and have no relation whatsoever to anyone bearing the same name or names. They are not even distantly inspired by any individual known or unknown to the author, and all the incidents are pure invention.

First published in Great Britain 2012
by Mills & Boon, an imprint of Harlequin (UK) Limited.
Harlequin (UK) Limited, Eton House, 18-24 Paradise Road,
Richmond, Surrey TW9 1SR

ISBN: 978 0 263 22659 1

Harleq
and re
forests
legal e

Printe
by CP

A NIGHT OF LIVING DANGEROUSLY

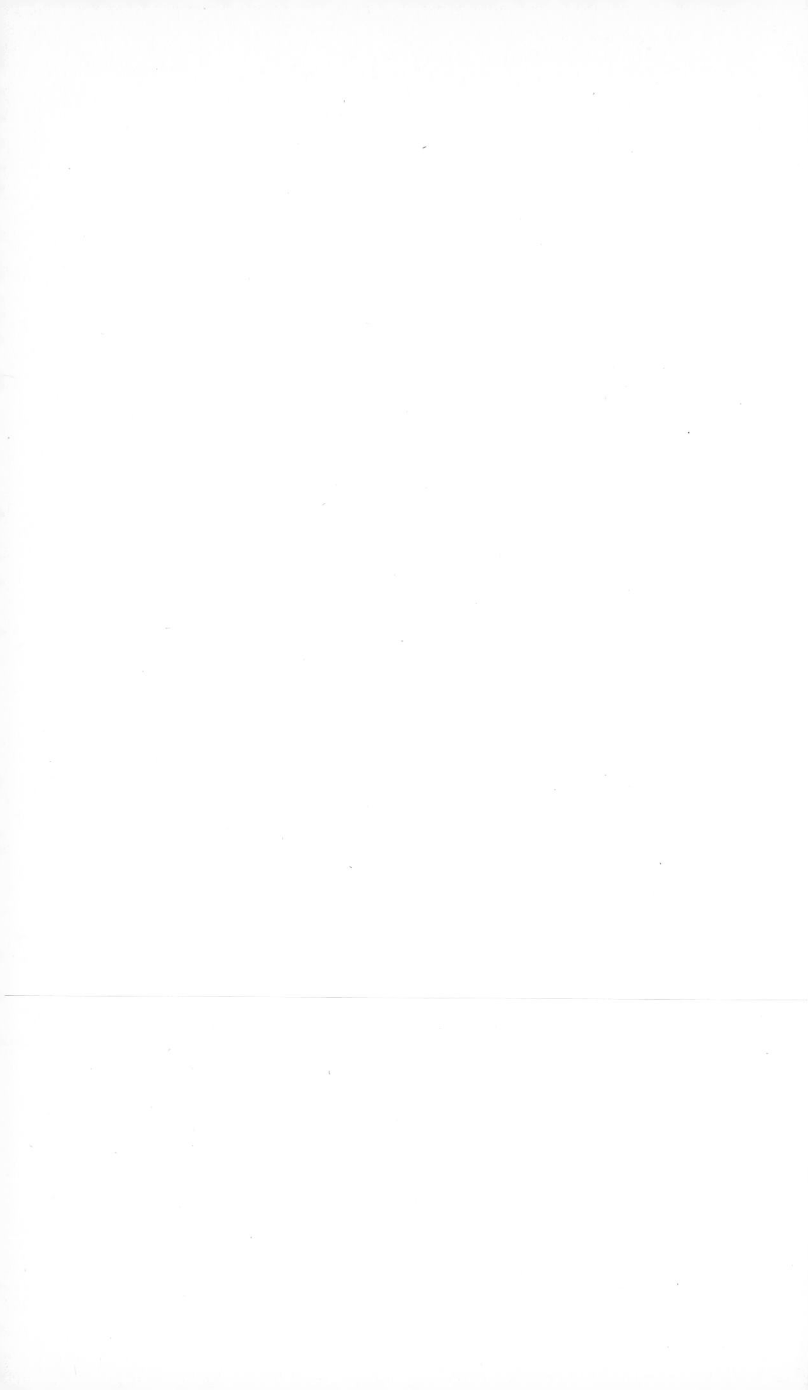

CHAPTER ONE

"Is someone here?"

The man's voice was harsh, echoing down the dark halls. Clapping a hand over her mouth, Lilley Smith cut herself off mid sob and ducked back farther into the shadows. It was Saturday evening, and except for the security guards in the lobby downstairs, she'd thought she was alone in the twenty-floor building. Until five seconds ago, when she'd heard the elevator ding and she'd dashed into the nearest private office to hide, dragging her file cart willy-nilly behind her.

Stretching out her foot, Lilley silently nudged the door closed. She wiped her puffy, tearstained eyes, trying not to make a sound as she waited for the man in the hall to leave so she could cry in peace.

Her day had been so horrible it was almost funny. Coming home that morning from an unfortunate, one-time-only attempt at jogging, she'd found her boyfriend in bed with her roommate. Then she'd lost her fledgling dream business. Finally, calling home for comfort, she'd been disinherited by her father. An impressive day, even for her.

Normally it would have bothered Lilley that she'd had to catch up with work on the weekend *again*. Today it didn't even register. She'd worked as a file clerk for Caetani Worldwide for two months, but it still took her twice as long as Nadia, the other file-room clerk, to get her files sorted, delivered and returned.

Nadia. Her co-worker, roommate and, as of this morning, former best friend. Exhaling, Lilley leaned back against her cart as she remembered the stricken look in Nadia's face as she'd tumbled out of bed with Jeremy. Covering herself with a robe, Nadia had cried and asked Lilley for forgiveness as Jeremy tried to make their betrayal sound like Lilley's fault.

Lilley had fled the apartment and gone straight for the bus downtown. Lost, desperate for comfort, she'd called her father for the first time in three years. That hadn't gone too well either.

Thank heaven for work. This job was all she had now. But when would the stranger in the hallway leave? When? She couldn't let him—or anyone—see her like this—with red puffy eyes, working at a snail's pace as every single letter and number shimmered and moved back and forth on the files. Who was the man, and why wasn't he dancing and drinking champagne at the charity ball with everyone else?

Lilley shivered. She'd never been in this office before, but it was cavernous and cold, with stark, expensively appointed furnishings of dark wood, a gorgeous Turkish carpet and floor-to-ceiling windows that revealed twilight across downtown San Francisco and the bay beyond. Her head slowly tilted back to view the frescoed ceilings. It was an office fit for a king. Fit for...

Fit for a prince.

Lilley's lips parted. Panic ripped through her as she realized for the first time whose office this had to be. She gave a terrified little squeak.

The office door creaked open. Lilley reacted on pure instinct, throwing herself through the shadows into the nearest closet.

"Who's in here?" The man's voice was harsh and low.

Heart pounding, she peered through the gap in the door. She saw the hulking silhouette of the stranger's broad-shouldered body in the dim light of the hall, blocking her only avenue of escape.

She covered her mouth with her hands, realizing she'd left her file cart behind the black leather sofa. All the man had to do was turn on the light and he'd see it. Being caught sobbing in the hallway would have been humiliating. Being caught skulking in the CEO's office would be a career-destroying disaster!

"Come out." The man's footstep was heavy on the floor. "I know you're in here."

Her heart stopped in her chest as she recognized that husky, accented voice. It wasn't some random janitor or junior assistant who was about to catch her. It was the CEO himself.

Tall, dark and broad-shouldered, Prince Alessandro Caetani was a self-made billionaire, the CEO of a luxury conglomerate that reached to every corner of the globe. He was also a ruthless playboy. All the women who worked in his San Francisco regional headquarters, from the youngest secretary to the fifty-something female vice president, were madly in love with him.

And now he was about to catch Lilley alone in his office.

Trying not to breathe, she backed farther into his closet, pressing her body behind his jackets, against the back wall. His suits smelled of sandalwood and musk and power. She closed her eyes, praying the prince would turn and leave. For once in her life, she prayed her skill at being invisible to men would actually pay off.

The door was ripped open. The jackets were shoved aside

as a large hand ruthlessly grabbed her wrist. She gave a little shriek as he pulled her out of the closet.

"I've got you now," he growled. He switched on a lamp, and a circle of golden light filled the dark, cavernous office. "You little..."

Then he saw her, and his black eyes widened with surprise. Lilley sucked in her breath as, against her will, she looked straight into the face of her boss for the first time.

Prince Alessandro Caetani was the most handsome man she'd ever seen, from his muscular body beneath his black tuxedo to the cold expression in his dark eyes. His aristocratic Roman nose was offset by the slightly thuggish curve of his sharp, dark-shadowed jawline. He looked—and was, if the legends were true—half prince, half conqueror.

"I know you." Prince Alessandro frowned, looking puzzled in the soft glow of the lamplight. "What are you doing here, little mouse?"

Her wrist burned where he touched her, sending sparks up her arm and down the length of her body. "What—what did you call me?"

He abruptly dropped her wrist. "What is your name?"

It took her a minute to remember. "L-Lilley," she managed. "From the file room."

Prince Alessandro's eyes narrowed. He walked around her, slowly looking her up and down. Her cheeks went hot. Compared to his gorgeous perfection in his sleek, sophisticated tuxedo, she knew she was frumpy and frightful in her sweatshirt and gray baggy sweatpants. "And what are you doing here, Lilley from the file room? Alone in my office on a Saturday night?"

She licked her dry lips, trying to calm her shaking knees. "I was...was..." What had she been doing, anyway? Where was she? Who was she? "I was just...um..." Her eyes fell on the file cart. "Working?"

He followed her gaze, then lifted a dark eyebrow. "Why are you not at the Preziosi ball?"

"I…I lost my date," she whispered.

"Funny." His sensual mouth curved in a humorless smile. "That seems to be going around."

The sexy, deep, accented timbre of his voice moved over her like a spell. She couldn't move or look away from his masculine beauty as he towered over her, strong, powerful and wide-shouldered, with thighs like tree trunks.

Thighs? Who said anything about his *thighs*?

Ever since Jeremy had arranged her file-room job, Lilley had done her best to make sure her billionaire boss never noticed her. And now, beneath the prince's black, hypnotic gaze, she found herself suddenly wanting to blurt out why. She wasn't very good at telling lies, not even white ones. The hot, searing depths in Prince Alessandro's dark eyes whispered that she could tell him anything, anything at all, and he would understand. He would forgive and show mercy.

But she'd been around powerful men before. She recognized the intensity of his gaze for what it actually was: an emotional shakedown.

The ruthless playboy prince, show mercy? No way. If he knew about Lilley's father, about her *cousin,* he'd fire her. Or worse.

"Lilley," he mused aloud in the silent office. He tilted his head, and his eyes suddenly gleamed in the small circle of lamplight. "What is your last name?"

"Smith," she said honestly, then hid a smile. No help for him there.

"And what are you doing in my office, Miss Smith?"

The scent of him, sandalwood and musk and soap and something more—something uniquely *him*—washed over her. She gave an involuntary shiver. "Returning, um, files."

"You know my files go to Mrs. Rutherford."

"Yes," she admitted unhappily.

He moved closer. She could practically feel the warmth of his body through his crisp black tuxedo jacket. "Tell me why you're really here."

She swallowed, looking down at the expensive carpet beneath her old, scuffed jogging shoes. "I just wanted to work for a few hours in peace and quiet. Without anyone bothering me."

"On a Saturday night?" he said coldly. "You were searching my office. Going through my files."

She looked up. "No!"

Prince Alessandro folded his arms. His dark eyes were hard, his expression like chiseled stone.

"I was hiding," she said in a voice almost too soft to hear.

"Hiding?" His voice was silky. "Hiding from what?"

Against her will, the truth was ripped out of her. "From you."

His dark eyes sharpened. He leaned forward. "Tell me why."

Lilley could barely even breathe, much less think, with Prince Alessandro Caetani so close to her.

The soft golden glow of the lamp, the darkening twilight outside the windows filled the enormous, high-ceilinged office with deepening shadows. "I was crying," she whispered over the lump in her throat. "I couldn't stay at home, I'm days behind on my work, and I didn't want you to see me because I was crying!"

Struggling not to cry, Lilley looked away. If she wept in front of her powerful boss, her humiliation would be complete. He would fire her—whether for skulking in his office, for crying in such an unprofessional way, or for being so behind on her work, it hardly mattered. She would lose the last thing she valued. The perfect finale to the second-worst day of her life.

"Ah," he said softly, looking down at her. "At last, I understand."

Her shoulders sagged. He was going to tell her to gather her things and get out of his building.

The prince's gaze was full of darkness, an ocean at midnight, deep enough to drown in. "You were in love with him?"

"What?" Lilley blinked. "Who?"

The corners of his sensual mouth curved upward. "The man."

"What makes you think I was crying over a man?"

"Why else would a woman weep?"

She laughed, but the sound was almost like a sob. "Everything has gone wrong today. I thought I might be happier if I lost some weight. I tried to go for a jog. Big mistake." She looked down at her old running shoes, at her baggy sweatshirt and sweatpants. "My roommate thought I'd left for work. When I came back to the apartment I found her with my boyfriend. In bed."

Alessandro cupped her cheek. "I'm sorry."

Lilley looked up at him, shocked by his unexpected sympathy. Then her lips parted. Sparks spread from his touch, zinging from her earlobes to her scalp, down her neck and spine, causing heat to whirl like lightning across her skin. Her breasts felt strangely heavy, her nipples tightening beneath her workout bra.

His eyes narrowed in surprise. "But you're beautiful."

Beautiful? It was like a slap in the face. She ripped away. "Don't."

He frowned. "Don't what?"

His cruelty took her breath away. She blinked fast, glaring up at him. "I know I'm not beautiful. And it's fine. I know I'm not smart either, and I can live with that. But for you to stand there and taunt me like that..." She gripped her hands into fists. "It's not just *patronizing*, it's heartless!"

Alessandro looked down at her gravely, not saying a word. And Lilley sucked in her breath, realizing she'd just told off her boss.

She clasped her hands together. "I'm fired, right?" When he didn't reply, a shudder of grief went through her. Her hands shook as she picked up a file from the floor and reached for the metal cart. "I'll finish my work," she said miserably, "then collect my things."

He grabbed her arm, stopping her. "So a compliment is a taunt?" Staring down at her, he shook his head. "You're a strange girl, Lilley Smith."

The way Prince Alessandro was looking at her, for an instant she'd almost thought—but no. *Strange* was a code word for *helpless failure*. She said over the lump in her throat, "So my father has always told me."

"You're not fired."

She looked up at him with the first glimmer of hope. "I'm not?"

Leaning forward, he took the file from her hand and set it on top of the metal cart. "I have a different sort of penalty in mind."

"The guillotine?" she said weakly. "The electric chair?"

"You'll come with me to the ball tonight."

Her lips fell open. "W-what?"

His dark eyes were as warm as molten chocolate and hot as embers of fire. "I want you to be my date."

Lilley stared at him, her eyes wide, her heart pounding. Had she fallen into some strange dream? Prince Alessandro could have the most beautiful women on earth—and he'd already had quite a few of them, according to the celebrity tabloids. Frowning, she turned around to make sure he wasn't talking to some movie star or lingerie model behind her.

"Well, *cara?*" he said huskily. "What do you say?"

Lilley turned back. She felt dizzy from his attention, half-drunk beneath the intensity of his dark gaze. She said slowly, "I don't understand."

"What's to understand?"

Lilley cleared her throat. "I don't get the joke."

"I never joke."

"You don't? Too bad. I joke all the time," she said. "Usually by accident."

He didn't even smile. He just looked down at her, his face unmovable and oh, so handsome.

"You're serious?"

"Yes."

"But—it's the Preziosi di Caetani ball," she stammered. "The biggest charity event of the summer. The mayor will be there. The governor. The paparazzi."

"So?"

"So you could have any woman you want."

"And I want you."

His four simple words made Lilley's heart twist in her chest. She clasped her trembling hands together. "But you have a girlfriend. I've read—"

His expression hardened. "No."

"But Olivia Bianchi—"

"No," he said tersely.

Biting her lip, Lilley looked up at him. He wasn't telling her the whole truth. And the waves of danger emanating off his body nearly scorched her. If he found out who Lilley really was, she would lose her job—or possibly get dragged into court on charges of corporate espionage. Every instinct of self-preservation told her one thing: *Run.*

"Sorry," she said. "No."

His eyes widened. She'd clearly shocked him. "Why?"

She bit her lip. "My work—"

"Give me a real reason," he bit out.

A real reason? How about the fact that she was the daughter of a man he hated, and the cousin of another man he hated even more? Or the biggest reason of all: his strength, power and masculine beauty terrified her, making her heart pound and her body break out in a hot sweat? No man had ever had this effect on her, ever, and she didn't know what to do. Except run.

"My boyfriend...my ex-boyfriend," she stumbled, "will be at the ball tonight with my friend—Nadia. So you see I couldn't possibly go."

"He'll be at the ball?" Alessandro's eyes sharpened. "Do I know him—this man who made you weep?"

"He works in the Preziosi jewelry-design division."

His eyes gleamed. "All the more reason to go. When he sees you on my arm, he will remember your value and beg you to come back to him. You can accept his groveling or spurn him, as you choose. And the woman will suffer when she sees you as my date."

She stared up at him in amazement. "You don't have self-esteem issues, do you?"

He looked at her with an even gaze. "We both know it is true."

Lilley pressed her lips together, knowing he was right. If she went as his date, she would be the most envied woman in the city—possibly in all of California.

The thought of Nadia and Jeremy groveling at her feet and begging for forgiveness was a delicious one. All the times Lilley had worked late, all the times she'd asked Nadia to please explain to Jeremy and entertain him, and they'd betrayed her. She had no friends in this city now. None.

She lifted her eyes to Alessandro's. "I'm not a very good dancer."

He slowly looked her over. "I find that hard to believe."

"I took ballroom-dancing lessons as a kid, and my teacher asked me to quit. I was like one of those dancing elephants with tutus. All my boyfriends have complained about me stepping on their feet."

His expression changed, became softer. "Even if that were true," he murmured, "the fault would be your partner's, not yours. It is the man's responsibility to lead."

She swallowed. "Um. I…I never thought of that. I just assumed I was to blame."

"You assumed wrong," he said simply, then lifted his eyebrow. "But just out of curiosity, how many is all?"

"What?"

"*All* your boyfriends."

Oh heavens. She couldn't tell him her pathetic number. She lifted her chin and said with false bravado, "A few."

"Ten?" he persisted.

The heat in her cheeks deepened as her shoulders slumped. "Two," she confessed. "A boyfriend in high school, and…" A lump rose in her throat. "…and Jeremy."

"Jeremy. That is his name? The man who broke your heart?"

"He betrayed me." She looked at the floor. "But that's not what broke my heart."

He waited, but she did not explain. "So go out tonight. Your dancing skills are irrelevant, because we will not dance."

She looked up at him with a crooked grin. "Afraid of getting your toes stomped?"

"I do not dance."

Her eyes widened. "What—never?"

"No."

"But you're the sponsor of the Preziosi di Caetani ball!"

"It raises money for my favorite charity and gets good press for Caetani Worldwide," he said coldly. "That's what I care about. Dancing does not interest me."

"Oh," Lilley said uncertainly. She bit her lip. "I see."

But she didn't see at all. How could a man like Prince Alessandro, the heartthrob of women around the world, sponsor a ball and not dance? It didn't make sense.

He started to reach for her hand. "Come. We must hurry."

She backed away. She was afraid to let him touch her again, afraid of his strange power over her body. She gulped. "Why me?"

"Why *not* you?"

Setting her jaw, she folded her arms. "You're famous for many things, Prince Alessandro, but taking file clerks on charity dates isn't one of them."

He threw back his head and laughed. Turning, he went to the large modernist painting above his desk and swung it open to reveal a safe. Turning the combination to open the door, he pulled out two platinum and diamond cufflinks, then faced her with new intrigue. "You interest me, Lilley Smith. Not one woman in a thousand would have asked me why before saying yes."

"I guess I'm weird that way." She watched him put on his expensive cufflinks one at a time, saw the strength of his wrists and the sensual movement of his hands. He paused.

"My date for the ball fell through ten minutes ago."

"Miss Bianchi?"

"Yes."

She'd seen pictures of the Milanese heiress, who was blond, thin and beautiful—everything Lilley was not. She looked down. "I'm nothing like her."

"That makes you perfect," he said harshly. "Olivia will

learn how I respond to ultimatums. I need a date, and I found you in my office. It is fate."

"Fate," she whispered. He came back around his desk, his body a dark, powerful shadow. His eyes locked with hers.

"I need a date. You need revenge. This Jeremy will be on his knees for you before the night is through."

A low current went up her spine. No matter how much they'd hurt her, she knew revenge was wrong. And being close to Alessandro scared her. She wasn't just afraid for her job. He made her feel so…so strange.

"Why do you hesitate?" he demanded. "Are you in love with him?"

She shook her head. "It's just…"

"What?"

Swallowing, she turned away. "Nothing."

"I've watched you for weeks, little mouse, trying to avoid me."

Her lips parted in shock. "You saw me?"

He gave a single nod. "Scurrying the other way when you saw me in the halls. This type of behavior from a woman is very…singular. It puzzled me. But now I understand."

"You do?" she croaked.

He touched her cheek, forcing her to meet his eyes. "Most women I've met would have deserted their lovers in an instant to be with me. Loyalty is a rare quality. This man who betrayed you, he is a fool."

She couldn't argue with that. She stared up at him, mesmerized.

He dropped his hand. "But you have nothing to fear," he said simply. "Our romance will be only an illusion. I will not call you tomorrow. I will not call you ever. After tonight, you will again be just my employee, and I will be your boss, pretending not to notice as you avoid me in the shadows."

Lilley swallowed, still feeling his touch on her cheek. "You mean if I go with you to the ball tonight," she whispered, "you'll ignore me tomorrow? You'll ignore me forever?"

"Yes."

Lilley exhaled. She had to make him forget her existence. It was the only way to guarantee he wouldn't be curious enough to discover the omissions on her résumé. But in her heart of hearts, she knew that wasn't the only reason.

You're always running away, Lilley. Jeremy's stinging indictment rang in her ears. *You said you came to San Francisco to pursue your jewelry business and spend time with me. Instead you've avoided us both since the day you arrived here. Either you never really wanted me or the business, or you're the worst coward I've ever known.*

Lilley closed her eyes. That morning, she'd been too angry to listen to his words. Jeremy and Nadia had betrayed her, pure and simple. She'd done nothing wrong. Right?

Right?

But suddenly all she wanted to do was prove Jeremy wrong. To be one of the glamorous, carefree, fearless girls who wore sparkly clothes and danced, laughed and drank champagne. To be the girl courted by a knight in shining armor.

To be the girl who attended a ball with a prince.

She wasn't a coward. She wasn't. She could be as brave and ruthless as anyone. She could watch Prince Alessandro and learn!

Lilley opened her eyes. "I accept."

He looked down at her. "Do you understand, Lilley?" he said evenly. "It's not a real date. There will be nothing between us tomorrow. Absolutely nothing."

"Yeah, I get it," she said. "Monday I'll go back to the file room. You'll go back to Rome and probably Miss Bianchi, when you're done teaching her your little lesson. I'll continue to work for you and you'll never bother me again. Perfect."

He stared at her, then snorted a laugh, shaking his head. "You continue to surprise me, Lilley," he murmured, wrapping his hand around her waist. "Come. We haven't much time."

As he led her out of the office, she felt a rush of sensation from the heaviness of his arm around her. Trying to ignore the wobble of her knees, she glanced back at the file cart. "But I haven't finished my work—"

"It will be arranged."

"And I don't have a dress!"

His lips curved. "You will."

She looked up at him, annoyed. "Who am I, Cinderella? Are you supposed to be my fairy godmother? I'm not going to let you buy me a dress!"

In the hallway, he pushed the button to summon the elevator then took her hand in his own. "Of course you will." He gently pushed some strands of brown hair out of her eyes. "You will let me do exactly as I please, and I will give you an evening of pleasure. A beautiful gown, the envy of your coworkers and revenge against the people who betrayed you. It will be…an interesting night."

Lilley breathed in his scent of clean skin and sandalwood, of seduction and power. She felt his palm against her own, rough and hot, and her pulse quickened, sending shivers up and down her virgin body. "All right. Yes."

His dark eyes gleamed in the shadows of the hallway. "Yes?"

"Yes to the dress. To your help." She licked her lips and

gave him a trembling smile. "Yes to everything, your highness."

"Call me Alessandro." He lifted her hand to his mouth. She felt the press of his smooth, sensual lips and the heat of his breath against her skin, and gasped as fire raced up her arm and down the length of her body, igniting her like a match thrown into gasoline. "And women always do," he murmured.

She licked her lips, dazed. "What?"

He straightened. His dark eyes were hot as a smile curled his sensual lips.

"Say yes," he whispered. "To everything."

CHAPTER TWO

EVENING fog had rolled in, seeping beneath Alessandro's tuxedo as he stepped out of the limo onto the red carpet outside the hundred-year-old mansion on Nob Hill. It was August, but the fog was clammy and damp against his skin, a cold wet slap across the face.

Alessandro was grateful. A cold slap was exactly what he needed at the moment.

Flashbulbs of the waiting paparazzi popped around him as he heard Lilley's high heels clack against the concrete then step softly onto the red carpet behind him. Alessandro's body tightened. Overwhelming desire crackled through his blood, a shocking need that had begun the moment he'd gotten his first real look at her face in his office.

And now it was a hundred times worse. Just the drive in the limo had been almost unbearable, as he sat beside her. *He hadn't known she was so beautiful.*

He felt Lilley's graceful arm wrap around his, felt the light, gentle pressure of her hand against his forearm, felt the warmth of her touch through his tuxedo jacket.

With a shiver of desire, he looked down at her.

He'd noticed the mousy file clerk weeks ago. Rosy-cheeked and brown-haired, always wearing shapeless, unattractive dresses, she'd looked barely more than twenty and fresh from the country. After watching her veer away from him in a panic with her cart whenever their paths crossed, he'd been curious enough to have Mrs. Rutherford pull a copy of the girl's file. But he hadn't discovered anything very interesting there. She'd moved to San Francisco in June, and the file-room position was apparently her first job since working as a hotel housekeeper in Minneapolis a few years ago. Everything about her was forgettable, even her name.

Except that was no longer true.

Alessandro exhaled. He'd intended to teach Olivia she could be replaced with anyone, even an unfashionable, plump, plain file clerk, fresh from the farm. But the joke was on him, it seemed.

How come he'd never really seen Lilley Smith until today?

Unfashionable? A personal stylist at a luxury boutique had poured Lilley into a long, slinky red dress with spaghetti straps. Backless and daringly low-cut, the red knit gown seemed to cling to her breasts, teasing a man's gaze, threatening at any moment to reveal too much.

Plump? The dress showed off the curves her baggy clothes had hidden. Her breasts and hips were generous and wide, her waist small. She had the shockingly feminine figure that used to drive men wild…and still did. The classic 1950s Marilyn Monroe curves that made any man break out in a sweat. A droplet formed on Alessandro's forehead just looking at her.

And plain? That was the biggest laugh of all. Alessandro had seen the rare beauty of her naked face up close in his office—but now, after Sergio's makeup and hair team had done their work, her loveliness was shocking. Kohl and mascara darkened her deep-brown eyes, and red lipstick highlighted the seductive curve of her full, generous mouth.

Lilley's long, light-brown hair tumbled seductively down her bare shoulders and naked back.

Alessandro had watched her for weeks from a distance, but it was only today that he'd finally seen Lilley Smith for what she truly was.

A beauty.

A sex kitten.

A *bombshell.*

As they walked down the red carpet towards the sweeping steps of the hundred-year-old Harts Mansion, the paparazzi went crazy, shouting questions.

"Where's Olivia? Did you two break up?"

"Who's the new girl?"

"Yeah, who's the sexy brunette?"

Alessandro gave them a half smile and a brusque wave. He was accustomed to being followed and photographed wherever he went, from his palace in Rome to his yacht in Sardinia to his North American headquarters in San Francisco. It was the price he paid for being successful and a bachelor. But as he led Lilley down the red carpet, her feet dragged behind him. He glanced down at her, and realized she was shaking.

"What is it?" he said beneath his breath.

"They're staring at me," she said in a low voice.

"Of course they're staring." Alessandro turned to her, brushing hair away from her eyes. "So am I."

"Just get me through this," she whispered, her beautiful brown eyes looking big and scared. His heart twisted strangely. Tucking her hand more securely around his arm, Alessandro led her swiftly down the red carpet, using his body to block the more aggressive photographers leaning over the ropes. Alessandro usually stopped for photographs—an unfortunate necessity to maximize publicity for the children's charity that would benefit tonight—but he knew Lilley would never manage. Ignoring the shouted questions and frustrated groans, he kept walking, leading her up the sweeping stairs to the shadowy columns of the portico.

Once they were inside the mansion's double doors, past security and into the golden, glittering foyer, Lilley exhaled. Her luminous eyes looked up at him with gratitude. "Thanks." She swallowed. "That was…not fun."

"No?" he said lightly. "Most women think otherwise. Most see it as a perk of dating me."

"Well, I don't." Lilley shuddered. She licked her lips, fidgeting with the low neckline of her tight red gown. "I feel like a dork."

Heat flashed through Alessandro. He wanted to touch everywhere her fingers were tugging, to rip the fabric off her body and cover those amazing breasts with his hands, to nibble and stroke and lick every inch of her.

No, he told himself angrily. He had three rules. No employees, no wives, no virgins. There were too many women in the world, all too easily possessed, to break those cardinal rules. Lilley was an employee. She was also brokenhearted and on the rebound. Too many complications. Too many risks. Lilley was off limits.

But then again…

Alessandro looked at the red fabric barely clinging to her breasts. Looked at the graceful curve of her neck, at the roses in her cheeks and her pale skin beneath thick waves of soft brown hair. He felt a rush of forbidden desire.

Maybe it was a stupid rule, he thought. Maybe taking an employee as his mistress was a great idea. Wasn't his HR department always telling him to promote from within?

Lilley's beautiful eyes looked miserable and vulnerable. "I look like an idiot, don't I?"

Didn't she realize her beauty? Why did she hide it? Why

didn't she use it to gain attention in the workplace to get ahead, as other women would have done?

Was it possible that she really didn't know how lovely she was? He narrowed his eyes. "You are beautiful, Lilley."

Looking up at him, she suddenly scowled, her lovely expression peeved. "I told you never to call me that—"

"You are beautiful," he said harshly, cupping his hand against her soft cheek. He searched her gaze. "Listen to me. You know the kind of man I am. The kind, you said, who would never take a girl on a charity date. So why would I lie? You are beautiful."

The anger slid from her face. She suddenly looked bewildered and innocent and painfully shy. He could read her feelings in her face, something else he found shocking. It was an act—right? It had to be. She couldn't be that young.

He'd been open-hearted and reckless too, long ago. He remembered it like some long-forgotten dream. Perhaps that was why he felt strangely, unexpectedly protective.

He didn't like it.

"You really—" Lilley stopped herself, then bit her lip. "You really think I'm pretty?"

"Pretty?" he demanded, amazed. Lifting her chin, he tilted her head up towards the light shining from the foyer's glittering chandelier. "You are a *beauty,* little mouse."

She stared up at him, then her lips suddenly quirked. "You keep calling me that. Can't you just call me Lilley?"

"Sorry." His lips curved. "It's a habit. It was my name for you, when I was blind."

Lilley's brown eyes sparkled as a smile lit up her face. "So in one breath you tell me I'm beautiful, and in the next you tell me you're blind?"

Her smile was so breathtaking that it caught at his heart.

"Your beauty would make any man blind, *cara,*" he said huskily. "I told you that you'd be envied if you came with me to the ball. I was wrong. *I* will be the one envied tonight."

Her eyes grew big, her dark eyelashes sweeping wide against her pale skin. "Huh. You're not so bad at this complimenting stuff." Her smile lifted into a wicked grin. "Has anyone ever told you that?"

Against his will, Alessandro grinned back at her, and as their eyes locked a seismic tremble raced through his body. How was it possible that he'd ever thought of Lilley as an invisible brown sparrow?

From the instant he'd seen her pushing her little filing cart down the hall, why hadn't he immediately seen her beauty? Lilley's combination of sweetness and tartness, her innocent eyes and lush, sexy curves, caused a spasm of need deeper than his body, down to some fundamental part of his soul.

Soul? The word made his lip curl. *Soul.* What a ridiculous idea. Funny the tricks lust could play on a man's mind.

And he wanted her. Oh yes.

But he wouldn't let himself act on it. He was not a slave to lust. He was a grown man, the head of a worldwide company, and it was past time that he stopped chasing one-night stands and settled down. Olivia Bianchi would make a perfect princess, and when she inherited her father's designer-clothing business, Caetani Worldwide's reach would double in Europe. He did not love her, any more than Olivia loved him, but their union made sense. He'd nearly talked himself into proposing until she'd pulled that little stunt.

He should have expected Olivia's ultimatum. He'd been on the phone in his limo, en route to the office for his forgotten cufflinks, and he'd felt her simmering beside him in her black fur coat. The instant he'd ended the business call, Olivia had turned on him in angry, rapid-fire Italian.

"When are you going to propose, Alessandro? When?

I'm sick of waiting for you to decide. Make our engagement official, or find someone else to be your hostess at the charity ball!"

Five minutes later, he'd dropped Olivia off at her ritzy hotel. No woman, not even one as powerful and perfect as Olivia, would ever give him an ultimatum.

Now, as Alessandro led Lilley towards the ballroom of the Harts Mansion, he felt a rush of relief that he was still a free man. This was already proving to be the most enjoyable, surprising night he'd had in a long time.

Keeping Lilley close beside him, he paused at the landing on the top of the stairs, looking down into the ballroom. A hush fell beneath the soaring painted ceilings and enormous crystal chandeliers as hundreds of guests turned to stare up at them. Alessandro felt Lilley stiffen. She wasn't accustomed to being the center of attention, that was certain. She seemed to expect criticism, which he could not remotely understand.

"I can't tell you you're beautiful, because you'll hit me," he murmured. "But I know every man would kill to be in my place."

Her eyes flashed up at him, and he saw her lips quirk into a nervous smile. "Okay," she said in a low voice, bracing herself. "Let's go."

Alessandro led her down the stairs, where his board members, stockholders and friends waited. He spoke to each of them in turn, then moved across the ballroom, greeting the mayor, the governor, movie stars and visiting royalty by name. The men grinned and asked him for stock tips. The women flirted with him and tossed their hair. And they all gaped at Lilley beside him. None of the upper-level directors of Caetani Worldwide recognized her, he was positive, though they'd likely passed her many times in the hallways.

Insane to think he'd once been just as blind.

Speaking with each of his guests in turn, Alessandro thanked them for their donation to his favorite children's charity. He felt Lilley trembling beside him as if she wanted to take flight, and took her hand firmly in his own, pressing her forward with a gentle push against the naked skin of her lower back. Even that innocent, courteous touch was incredibly erotic. All he wanted to do was leave the gala ball and drag Lilley away to some quiet place. Perhaps his villa in Sonoma, which conveniently had ten bedrooms.

"Your highness," the head of the children's charity said breathlessly, looking up at him through her glasses with dazzled eyes, "won't you say a few words to start the bidding for the auction tonight?"

"Certainly," Alessandro said with a practiced smile. "I'll do it at once."

Gripping Lilley's hand, he crossed the ballroom towards the stage, and the crowds parted for them like magic. He felt her panic as he led her up the stairs, felt her small hand pulling desperately to be freed. It was only once they were behind the wings of the stage that he released her hand, looking down at her.

"Thanks for being my date tonight," he said huskily, and leaned forward to kiss her cheek. It was just an innocent, friendly kiss. Practically nothing. But when he pulled away, her eyes were huge.

His own lips burned where they'd touched her skin. For an instant, they just stared at each other. His blood roared in his ears, his heart pounding with the need to pull her into his arms and kiss her, really kiss her. He had to force himself to step back.

"Excuse me." Years of not showing feelings stood him in good stead. His voice was calm and even, betraying nothing of his tumult within. "This will take just a moment."

"Sure," she said faintly.

Leaving her in the wings, he walked to the microphone at the center of the stage. A hush fell across the ballroom, and Alessandro waited for the hearty cheer of the crowd which quickly followed. He was accustomed to being the center of attention, and far from being nervous, he was bored by it—all of it. There was only one thing that did not bore him right now, one thing that made his blood hum and his body come alive. One thing he wanted.

And he could not let himself have her.

Gripping the podium with his hands, he gave a speech, hardly knowing what he was saying. He could feel Lilley watching from the wings. His heartbeat was quick, his body hot with repressed desire.

"...and so I thank you, my friends," he finished. "Drink champagne, dance and bid high. Remember every penny raised tonight goes to help children in need!"

The cheer across the ballroom was even louder. With an absentminded wave, he left the podium and went straight back to Lilley, who looked as if she'd recovered her senses and was now staring at her watch, keeping time.

"Six minutes." She looked up at him with quirked lips. "I'm impressed. Usually speeches given by important men last for at least an hour. You're fast."

He gave her a lazy smile, then leaned forward to whisper, "I'm slow where it counts."

Alessandro had the satisfaction of seeing her shiver. That was some solace, at least—knowing she was as aware of him as he was of her. It amazed him, how Lilley hid nothing of her feelings. So young, he thought in wonder, so reckless and unrestrained. It reminded him of what he'd once been like himself, before he'd been betrayed. Like her, he'd once been young and hopeful, poor and driven to succeed...

Poor? The sparkle of Lilley's watch caught his eye, and he grabbed her wrist. "What's this?"

She tried to pull her wrist from his grasp. "Nothing."

In the background, he could hear the orchestra start a waltz. He was dimly aware of guests going out to the dance floor. "It's platinum. Diamonds. I don't recognize the brand."

"Hainsbury," she said in a small voice.

Hainsbury's. The damned discount jewelry chain that had recently tried—and failed—to execute a hostile takeover of Caetani Worldwide, solely in order to acquire the cachet of his luxury jewelry brand, Preziosi di Caetani. His eyes narrowed. "Who gave it to you?"

She swallowed. "My mother."

He told himself it was entirely reasonable that someone from the Midwest might own a Hainsbury watch. It was a coincidence, nothing more. His endless battles with the Count of Castelnau, his crafty, vicious French rival, were making him paranoid. He looked at Lilley's face. Clearly he was losing his mind to be suspicious of a girl like this.

"Nice," he said casually, dropping her wrist. "I wouldn't have recognized it. It looks nothing like their usual factory-made junk."

Looking away, she wrapped her hand around her wrist. Her voice was awkward. "My mother had it specially made."

He'd embarrassed her, Alessandro thought. Drawing attention to her Hainsbury-brand watch at a ball sponsored by the far more prestigious Preziosi di Caetani. "Whoever made it, your watch is truly exquisite." He smiled down at her and changed the subject. "Had enough of the ball? Ready to leave?"

"Leave?" Her lips parted. "We just got here!"

"So?" he said impatiently.

She glanced uneasily towards the dance floor. "People are waiting to talk to you."

"They already have my money."

"It's not just a question of money. They clearly want you. Your time and attention." She gave him a sudden crooked smile. "Though heaven knows why. I've yet to see your charm myself."

He gave her a sensual smile. "Do you want me to try harder?"

Her eyes widened and he heard her intake of breath. She muttered, "I'm no good at this."

"To the contrary."

She shook her head. "Forget it. Just don't try to charm me, all right? There's no point, and it might…I mean…we're just using each other tonight. Leave it at that."

Alessandro's gaze fell to her trembling lips. "Right. You're here for revenge. You haven't seen him yet, have you?"

"No." Her voice was quiet.

"He will fall on his knees when he sees you," Alessandro said roughly. "Come."

Grabbing her hand, he led her off the stage and across the dance floor, tracing through the crowds of swaying, laughing couples. Once, Alessandro would have been the first man on the dance floor. He would have pulled Lilley into his arms and moved her against his body in the music's seductive rhythm. But he hadn't danced for sixteen years now. Crossing the floor, he didn't even pause.

The charity director waited for him on the other edge of the dance floor. She beamed at him, gushing thanks and praise, and Alessandro accepted her gratitude with as much grace as he could manage. He was glad to help the charity, but the long line of guests that instantly formed, people waiting to thank him and shake his hand, seemed endless. Almost beyond endurance. He wanted to grab Lilley's hand and jump into his car, and not stop until they were completely alone, away from the crowds of reaching hands and yearning eyes.

But there were some duties from which neither royalty nor wealth excused a man. Standing on the edge of the dance floor like a king holding court, he endured the long queue of wealthy donors and powerful people as best as he could. As solace, he pulled Lilley to stand in front of him, wrapping his arms around her as if he were a child with a comforting blanket.

Except he was no longer a child, and Alessandro had a grown man's idea of comfort. Throughout the endless small talk he found himself distracted by the way her full breasts felt, pressed against his arms. He allowed himself one glance down, and saw that her low neckline barely covered the indecent swell of her breasts. He could see the shape of pebbled nipples though the red knit fabric. It was just as he'd suspected—she wasn't wearing a bra. And he wasn't the only man to notice. All the eyes of the male guests waiting to talk to him lingered long upon her, and Alessandro felt an urge to growl at them.

He was long past hard. He had the sudden bright idea of writing the charity a ten-million-dollar check, if it meant he could leave this ball and take her straight to bed.

He shouldn't. He couldn't. Sex with Lilley was a bad idea on every level. She was his employee, possibly in love with another man, and she was right—they were using each other tonight for mutual gain. He'd told her that straight out. A cheap one-night stand would only end in her recriminations, tears and perhaps a sexual-harassment lawsuit.

But with every passing moment, his self-restraint was growing frayed. Feeling her in his arms right now he felt oddly alive in a way he hadn't experienced in years. She made him feel…young again. As if he still had a beating heart.

And *that* was her biggest danger of all. He couldn't seduce her. He had to send her away. Had to—

Lilley glanced back at him, her lips parted. He saw the tip of her pink tongue dart out to the edge of her mouth and he nearly groaned. He wanted to taste those lips. Plunder her mouth with his. He wanted to rip the clingy red dress off her body, to spread her across his bed, to push himself inside her, to fill her hard and deep—

Basta. He broke out into a hot sweat. As the ambassador droned on to him about the fluidity of Asian exchange rates, all Alessandro could think was that it was a good thing Lilley was standing in front of him, blocking others' view of his trousers. Where was his self-control?

In front of him, Lilley stiffened. For a moment, Alessandro wondered if she'd felt his desire for her—how could she not? Then he saw she was looking over the crowd.

"Jeremy," she said in a low voice.

For a moment, Alessandro couldn't remember what she was talking about. Then his insides burned. He felt envious of this employee in his jewelry-design department, this man who'd had her at his command and let her go.

"Excuse us," he said to the people surrounding them. Ignoring their protests, he pulled Lilley to a quiet corner next to a window.

"Where is he?" he said, keeping his expression impassive.

"Over there."

He followed her gaze. His eyes narrowed in the desire to see this paragon but no one stood out to him at all. He felt irritated. *Irritated* wasn't a strong enough word. *Jealous?* No, impossible. Jealousy was for the weak, for sad, vulnerable men who served their hearts on platters to be shredded and devoured.

So he didn't feel jealous. He felt...annoyed. *Sì.* Annoyed.

He'd said he would help Lilley get the man back. Now he regretted his promise. Why should he help another, less-deserving man get what he himself wanted—Lilley in his bed?

But if Lilley truly loved this Jeremy, Alessandro would do the honorable thing. He would step aside with the noble self-sacrifice of a damned saint.

"Va bene," he ground out. "If you still want this idiot, this imbecile without a shred of sense or loyalty, I will help you win him."

Lilley flashed him a grin. "Um. You're too kind?"

"Just tell me one thing," he demanded.

"Only one?"

His fingers moved down her shoulders, stroking down the warm, bare skin of her back. He saw her eyes widen, felt her shiver and he fought back the urge to yank her body hot and hard against his own. "Why would you want him back, after he made you weep?"

Her smile fell. She took a deep breath, then lifted her left wrist. "Look at this."

A change of subject? He looked down at the bracelet on her wrist. He'd noticed it earlier, a pastiche of welded materials—colorful crystals on a brass chain, interspersed with rusty-looking numbers and held together with a tarnished buckle. "What about it?"

"I made it."

He grabbed her wrist, narrowing his eyes and tilting his head as he tried to make sense of the bracelet. He pointed to the metal number dangling off the chain. "What's that?"

"A room number from an eighteenth-century Parisian hotel."

It seemed strange to him, an artistic hodgepodge of junk. "How do you source the materials?"

"At flea markets and vintage shops, mostly. I create jewelry using old things I find." She swallowed. "I met Jeremy at San Francisco's trade show a few months ago, when my employer thought I was visiting my family. Jeremy loved my jewelry. We decided to be partners and open a boutique together. He was going to handle the financials. I would create the inventory." She blinked fast, and looked away. "When he chose my roommate over me, I lost that dream."

He could see her eyes were shiny with tears, and his insides gave a little twist. "The man's a damned fool," he said roughly. He tried to think of how to comfort her. "Perhaps it's for the best," he tried. "Running a business is a huge risk. You might have lost your investment. People don't want old trinkets. They want their jewelry shiny and new."

Her lips trembled, curving as she looked up. Her eyes were bleak. "I guess we'll never know, will we?"

His attempt at comfort was a clear failure. But Alessandro knew words weren't enough to make anyone forget the loss of a dream. He had no idea how to make Lilley forget her pain. He knew only one way, the same way he used to forget his own.

But he couldn't do it. He couldn't allow himself to make love to her.

The orchestra started a new song, and the notes of an exquisite classical waltz swirled around them like cherry blossoms tumbling from the sky. Lilley looked out at the crowded dance floor wistfully.

She'd told him she wasn't a good dancer, but he didn't believe that for an instant. He'd seen the sensual way she moved. Even walking, her body swayed like sunset against ocean waves.

But he couldn't dance with her. His hands tightened at his sides. He was helpless to offer comfort.

Unless he made love to her.

What could it hurt? His lust argued against his brain.

One night of pleasure. A few hours of comfort. One night wouldn't risk making her fall in love with him. It wasn't as if she were a virgin.

Although she was shockingly close. *Two boyfriends.* He still couldn't believe she'd only been with two men. She truly was innocent. And yet she'd seemed embarrassed of her number. He wondered what she would think if he told her how many women he'd slept with. Something he would never do, even if he knew the number.

"I'm sorry I don't dance," he said slowly.

She looked down. "It's all right."

The scent of her hair was like wild roses. He moved closer, fascinated by the swoop of her neck, by the snub edge of her chin. Her cheeks blushed a soft pink against creamy skin as her dark eyelashes fluttered. He asked suddenly, "How old are you, Lilley?"

"Twenty-three." She furrowed her brow. "Why? How old are you?"

"Ancient to you. Thirty-five."

"Thirty-five, and still not married?" She sounded as astonished as his shareholders. "Where I come from, most people are married by thirty."

"Advantageous for farm life, I assume."

Her brow furrowed. "I don't exactly come from a—"

"In my world," he interrupted, "a man marries to ensure his line, to make sure he has a son to inherit his title and estate when he's dead."

She flashed him a grin. "Gee, you make it all sound so romantic."

"It's not about *romance,* Lilley," he said sharply. "Marriage is an alliance. My wife will be a leader in society. An heiress with proper lineage, the future mother to my heir."

Her grin faded. "Like Olivia Bianchi."

Even hearing her name irritated him. "Yes."

Lilley's eyes were huge beneath the glittering light of the chandeliers. "So if she's the perfect bride for you, why am I here?"

"She threatened to leave if I didn't propose, so I told her to go."

Lilley blinked. "I feel sorry for her."

He barked a laugh. "Do not waste your sympathy on Olivia. She can take care of herself."

"She's in love with you!" She swallowed. "It was wrong of me to agree to this—this charade. When you're just trying to control her."

"I have no desire ever to see Olivia again," he bit out.

She frowned, clearly unconvinced. "When did you decide that?"

His eyes met hers. "I knew it from the moment I saw you in that dress."

Her lips parted in shock. It took her several moments to speak. "Um. Would you get me a drink?" she croaked. "And maybe some food? I haven't eaten all day."

"Certamente," he murmured. "What would you like? A martini? A merlot?"

"You choose."

"We'll start with champagne." Reaching out a hand, he cupped her cheek. "Wait here, if you please, *cara*."

He felt her shiver beneath his touch, saw her lick her lips as she said with a trembling voice, "I'll wait."

He turned away, but after a few steps could not resist looking back at her. Lilley stood frozen on the edge of the dance floor, gloriously alluring in her red dress, watching him. She was surrounded by men who were already darting her greedy sideways glances.

Damned vultures. Alessandro scowled. He would hurry.

As he strode across the ballroom, he couldn't remember the last time he'd felt such need to possess any woman.

And he could have her. She was free and ripe for the taking. Yes, she was his employee, but he was the one who'd made that rule. He was the boss. He could break his own rules at will.

Alessandro thought again of the ten bedrooms at his villa. An image floated through his mind of Lilley spread naked on his bed, her full, generous mouth curved into a sensual smile, her deep-brown eyes looking up at him with a haze of longing and need. He nearly stumbled over his own feet.

And just like that, his decision was made. His body tightened as exhilaration raced through him. Employee or not, Lilley would be his.

Tonight. He would have her in his bed tonight.

CHAPTER THREE

LILLEY felt men in tuxedos jostle her on the edge of the dance floor, felt the annoyed glare of chic, half-starved women in black designer gowns around her. She took a deep breath, trying to steady her shaking hands. Alessandro's dark head towered above the crowds as he strode towards the bar, trailed by wide-eyed, adoring groupies.

And she was rapidly becoming one of them. Lilley exhaled. What in heaven's name was she doing? He'd told her outright that their date would only be an illusion. And yet, all night, Alessandro's eyes, his touch, had told her differently. Her body felt hot, her skin flushed and pink at the memory of his fingertips stroking her bare back. Of his fingers running lightly along her arm, his lips brushing her cheek.

Just being around him made her feel like a different woman. A bolder, braver one.

She didn't know why or how. Maybe it was the way he looked at her. The way his hard, muscular body felt against her own. Maybe it was his scent, like exotic lands and spice and sunshine. He made her feel tense and tingly and hot, and made her soul feel all jumbled and confused.

He made her feel a hunger she'd never known, and every moment she was near him, the hunger grew.

Lilley swallowed, rubbing her tense neck. She just had

to make it through the night. She'd keep her distance, keep her mouth shut, have some dinner and drink champagne for a couple of hours. Surely she could manage that? And tomorrow, it would all be nothing but a dream. On Monday she could go back to the file room, and Prince Alessandro Caetani would forget her existence.

She couldn't possibly believe his interest in her could be real. There was no way on the green earth that Alessandro would choose Lilley over Olivia Bianchi.

I have no desire ever to see Olivia again. She heard the echo of his husky voice. *I knew it from the moment I saw you in that dress.*

An electric current coursed through her body at the memory. She couldn't forget how he'd pulled her close, wrapping his arms around her as he spoke to politicians and football stars. She couldn't forget how his hot gaze had slowly perused the length of her body when they'd left the boutique, or the way he'd protected her past the paparazzi. A strange new tension had consumed her all night, causing her heart to beat too fast and her breasts to rise and fall in quick, shallow breaths against the snug bodice of her gown.

Maybe it was a good thing Alessandro didn't dance after all. If she felt his hard body swaying against hers, she might have hyperventilated and fallen like a stone on the dance floor. Every time their eyes met, every time he touched her, Lilley wanted things she could barely confess, even to herself.

"Lilley?"

Jeremy stood in front of her, his mouth agape at her tight red dress. He pushed up his black-framed glasses. "What are you doing here?"

"Oh. Hi Jeremy," Lilley said weakly. Licking her lips, she glanced at the black-haired woman behind him. "Hi, Nadia."

Her roommate's face was the picture of misery. She looked as if she were about to burst into tears. "I'm so sorry, Lilley," she choked out. "We never meant to hurt you. We never meant…"

"Stop apologizing," Jeremy told her. His Adam's apple bobbed over his bow tie as he glared at Lilley. "We would have told you days ago, if you'd let us. But you've avoided us. Avoided *me*."

Lilley's mouth had fallen open. "That's ridiculous!"

"I wish you'd just had the guts to tell me from the start you didn't want me, rather than pawning me off on Nadia. Is it any wonder we fell for each other? You were never there!"

Lilley shook her head fiercely. "You're just making excuses. You know I had to work! You're entirely to blame!"

His gaze met hers. "Am I?" His eyes traveled down her full, bouncy hair to the knit dress clinging to her breasts. "You sure never dressed like that for me. You're clearly here with someone you actually care about. Who is he, Lilley?"

It was time for her to lower the boom. Time to get revenge for their betrayal. As soon as she told them her date was Alessandro, they'd be shocked and jealous. Lilley opened her lips.

Then she saw Jeremy's hand on the small of Nadia's back.

It was a protective gesture, one Lilley had resisted every time Jeremy had tried to touch her. The truth was that, after one fun weekend at the trade show, their relationship had always been strained. She'd quit her job in France and moved to San Francisco to start this big new life, but she hadn't done anything to pursue her dreams. When Jeremy had tried to kiss her, she'd pulled away. She'd avoided being with him, coming up with excuses to stay at work a little longer. Looking back at their relationship, Lilley couldn't blame him for wanting to be with Nadia, a girl who actually had time for him, and who, as she'd seen to her shock that morning, actually seemed to relish his kisses.

She'd never loved him. The truth was, what hurt the most was losing her dream of the boutique. She couldn't start a business without Jeremy, she didn't have the remotest idea how to create a business plan or legally register her company or build a clientele. All she knew how to do was design jewelry that was funny and weird and definitely not for everyone.

She'd had such big dreams. And when he'd broken up with her, he'd ended them.

No. She'd done that herself, by never lifting a finger to pursue them.

"Who's your date, Lilley?" Nadia said hopefully through her tears. "Have you met someone?"

Maybe Jeremy had cheated on her, but she'd abandoned and rejected him for months. Maybe Nadia had taken her boyfriend behind her back—but hadn't Lilley begged her roommate to please, please make her excuses to Jeremy as she scurried off to work?

They'd been wrong. But Lilley had been a coward from start to finish.

Trembling, Lilley faced them. "I'm here with…with…" She swallowed, then lifted her chin. "A friend. I'm here with a new friend."

She turned to Jeremy.

"And you were right," she said. "I was never there. Not for you. And not for our business. I had all these dreams, but I was afraid even to try. I'm—I'm sorry."

Jeremy blinked, and the angry light in his eyes faded. "I'm sorry too," he said. "You're a nice person, Lilley, sweet and generous. You didn't deserve to find out about Nadia and me that way." He gave her an awkward smile. "I always liked you. But after you moved to San Francisco, you just…disappeared."

"I know." Her throat hurt. Every time Jeremy had made an appointment for them—at a bank, with a potential investor, with a real estate agent—she'd suddenly had somewhere else to be. She'd hidden behind her work. Her fear had won. "I'm sorry."

"Can you ever forgive me, Lilley?" Nadia whispered.

Lilley tried to smile. "Maybe if you do the dishes for the rest of the month."

"I will. Two months. Three!"

"And I'm sorry the boutique didn't work out." Jeremy rubbed the back of his sandy-blond head sheepishly. "I still think your jewelry is fantastic. You're just not ready to take the plunge. But maybe someday…"

"Right," she said over the lump in her throat, knowing it was a lie. "Someday."

Her roommate was openly crying as she leaned forward and hugged Lilley, whispering, "Thank you."

Lilley's throat hurt as she watched Jeremy and Nadia disappear into the crowd. Then she heard a dark, sardonic voice behind her.

"You didn't tell them about me."

She whirled around. "Alessandro."

"I was waiting to see you take your revenge." His tall, muscular body moved with a warrior's grace as he held out a flute of champagne. "Why didn't you tell them?"

"Because Jeremy was right. I never wanted him. Not really." She took the champagne flute from his hand and said softly, "If I don't have the guts to pursue my dreams, I shouldn't be angry if other people do."

"You could have made them suffer." His dark eyes were puzzled, almost bewildered. "I don't understand."

"That makes two of us," she whispered, and took a long

drink of champagne. The bubbles were a cold shock against her lips as she tilted back her head, gulping it all down. She closed her eyes, waiting for the alcohol to reach her brain and make her forget how she'd been so afraid to risk failure that she'd made it a self-fulfilling prophecy.

What was the point in her avoiding risk, if she ended up losing everything anyway?

"You're crying." Alessandro sounded aghast.

She exhaled, wiping her eyes. "No."

"I saw his face when he looked at you. He could still be yours for the taking, if you chose."

Lilley thought of the stricken expression on Nadia's face. Thought of the way Jeremy's hand had lingered protectively on her roommate's back. Thought of the way Lilley had never, not for one instant, felt a single spark of physical attraction for Jeremy—something she'd never even noticed until she'd experienced the lightning sizzle of electricity with Alessandro.

She shook her head. "I wish them all the best."

"God, you are so nice," he whispered, pushing back wavy tendrils of her hair. "How can you be so—merciful?"

An unexpected bolt of pain went through her. Another man calling her *nice.* Another word for *timid. Terrified. Coward.* No wonder Alessandro had called her little mouse.

Blinking fast, she looked down at her scandalous red dress and sexy high heels. "Do you think I'm a coward?" she whispered.

"What are you talking about?" Taking her empty flute, he pressed his own full glass into her hand. "Here. Drink this."

She looked up at him, her eyes full of unshed tears. "I shouldn't have said that aloud. You must think—"

"I think nothing." His dark gaze seared through her soul. "Never apologize for telling me what you're thinking. You can't hurt me. There is nothing between us, so you risk nothing."

She blinked at him, feeling quivery. "Now you're the one who is being nice."

He snorted, then shook his head, a small smile playing on his sensual mouth. "That is one accusation I've never heard before. Now drink."

Obediently, she took a sip. As she drank, she heard him muse aloud, "Delicious, isn't it? I just bought the winery from a Brazilian. Cost me a fortune." His lips curved. "But it gives me a great deal of pleasure, since I know it infuriates my worst enemy."

Lilley's eyes flew open as she pulled the flute from her lips. She said faintly, "Not the St. Raphaël vineyard."

"Ah, you recognize it?" He smiled in satisfaction. "It once belonged to the Count of Castelnau. Now it is mine."

"You don't say," Lilley said faintly, feeling sick. She'd heard Théo, her cousin and former employer, rage about losing that vineyard in a business deal to a Brazilian. It was only after he'd lost it that he'd realized its value. Typical, she thought. People were so much better at pursuing things they didn't need instead of enjoying what they already had.

But the two men had competed over acquisitions with growing ferocity for the last five years, ever since Théo had bought a small Italian luxury firm that Alessandro considered rightfully his by geography. If he ever found out she was Théo's cousin, he'd never believe Lilley wasn't a corporate spy. Especially after catching her in his office, all alone in the dark!

Her knees trembled. He caught her. "Are you all right?" he asked, looking concerned. "Did you drink the champagne too quickly?"

She looked up at him. She'd left her father's and cousin's names off her résumé because she'd known Caetani

Worldwide would have never hired her otherwise, in spite of Jeremy's recommendation, no matter how honest or hard-working she might be. But telling Alessandro the truth would gain her nothing, and would cost her her job—forcing her to go home to her father and perhaps even consider his demand that she marry his employee, a man twice her age.

"Lilley?"

"I just need something to eat," she managed. "I haven't eaten all day." She gave him a weak smile. "And I did jog a half mile."

"Of course." Taking the half-finished flute from her hands, he set both glasses on the silver tray of a passing waiter and gave her a sudden grin. "I've arranged for a private dinner of sorts. My driver has taken a selection from the buffet to the limo. We'll enjoy a little picnic on the way home."

"A picnic? In your limo?" she said faintly. She shook her head, feeling dizzy in a way that had nothing to do with champagne. With a wistful sigh, she looked back at the glamorous ballroom. "All right. I just—didn't expect it all to end so quickly."

"All good things come to an end," he said, holding out his hand.

Reluctantly, she took it. He led her across the ballroom, stopping many times to say farewell to his friends and admirers before they finally escaped up the stairs, through the foyer and out the double doors.

Outside, beneath the hundred-year-old mansion's shadowy portico, the August night was foggy and cold. "It must be midnight," she murmured.

"Almost. How did you know?"

"Because all night I've felt like Cinderella." She looked up at him, and gratitude, real gratitude, rose above her regret that the night was over. "Thank you for the best night of my life."

He blinked, then frowned. Abruptly, he pushed her against a white stone column. She shivered as she felt the cold, hard stone against the hot skin of her back.

"I don't think you understand," he said in a low voice. "I'm not taking you to *your* home." He paused. "I'm taking you to mine."

She stared at him in shock, hearing only her own hoarse breath and the rapid beat of her heart.

"You're my employee. There are rules." Alessandro's eyes were dark with heat, his dark hair dappled with streaks of silvery moonlight as he held her beneath the shadows of the portico. "But I'm going to break them," he whispered. "I'm going to kiss you."

Staring up at him, Lilley felt as though she was lost in a strange dream. Tendrils of hair whipped across her face; the fabric of her dress moved languorously against her thighs.

"All night I've thought of nothing but touching you." His hands moved down her shoulders to her naked back. He lowered his head to her ear, and she felt his lips brush her tender flesh. "If you want me to stop, tell me now."

She closed her eyes as she felt the warmth of his fingers stroke her bare skin, felt his powerful body, barely constrained by his civilized tuxedo, against her own. His fingertips stroked up her neck, and he tilted her head upwards, his face just inches away. She shivered, her lips parted. The two of them were alone in the foggy, moonlit world.

Then she heard paparazzi yapping like small dogs from the curb, barking out questions that were muffled by a sudden howl of cold wind. He twisted away from her sharply. Moonlight caressed the hard edges of his face, making him look like a dark avenging angel as he scowled behind them. He grabbed her wrist.

"Come on."

He pulled her down the stone steps, past the shouts and flashbulbs of the paparazzi and the reporters who screamed questions and lunged for Lilley as they passed. Alessandro knocked them aside with his powerful arm, gently pushing her into the waiting limousine before he slammed the door behind them.

"Drive," he ordered the chauffeur.

The uniformed driver gunned the engine, roaring away from the curb and plummeting down the steep San Francisco hill. Lilley exhaled as she looked through the window behind them. "Are they always like that?"

"Yes. Take the alleys," Alessandro said. "In case they follow."

"Of course, sir. The penthouse?"

"Sonoma." Alessandro replied, rolling up the privacy divider.

"Sonoma?" Lilley echoed.

He turned to her with a sensual, heavy-lidded smile. "I have a villa. It will give us complete privacy."

She swallowed. This was all happening so fast. "I don't know..."

He gave her a wicked half grin. "I swear I'll have you back in the city safe and sound before work on Monday."

Work! As if that was what she was worried about! Exhaling, Lilley noticed two plates of delicious food and white wine chilling in a bucket of ice. As the divider closed with a thunk, blocking off the driver's view of the back seat, she looked nervously at Alessandro. She'd been starving for hours, but suddenly dinner was the last thing on her mind.

Smiling, he put his hand on her cheek. She could see slivers of silvery light reflected in his fathomless black eyes as he whispered, "I thought a woman like you existed only in dreams."

Her shoulders stiffened. "You mean *nice?*" She felt a sudden lump in her throat. *"Sweet?"*

He gave a low laugh. "You have a way of turning my every compliment into an insult. But yes. You are those things." His hand slowly trailed down her neck, his fingertips stroking the sensitive corner of her shoulder, the hollow of her collarbone. "But that's not why I'm taking you home."

"It isn't?" she breathed.

"I want you in my bed." His gaze was hot. His thumb stroked her sensitive bottom lip, and sparks flashed up and down the length of her body. "I've never wanted any woman this much. I want to taste your mouth. Taste your breasts. To feel your body against mine and fill you until you weep with joy. I won't stop until I am satisfied." He stroked her jawline, tilting her face upward as he whispered, "Until *you* are satisfied."

She trembled, hardly able to breathe. His mouth was inches from hers, and her lower lip fell swollen, burning where he'd touched her. She could feel the warmth of his breath against her skin. Unconsciously, she tilted her head back, lifting her mouth a millimeter closer to his.

His hand slid down her neck, past her bare shoulder. "I offer you a night of pleasure. Nothing more." His palm caressed the length of her arm to the vulnerable pulse inside her wrist. "And nothing less."

Her heart pounded in her throat. She had to refuse him. *Had* to. She couldn't possibly toddle off to his villa in Sonoma and give her boss her virginity. There were a million reasons why this was a bad idea.

But her body refused to heed her brain. She felt as if she was spiraling out of control. She craved his darkness. Craved his fire. "A woman would have to be a fool," she breathed, "to get involved with a man like you."

The ghost of a smile haunted Alessandro's cruel, sensual mouth. He cupped her face with both hands.

"We all must choose in this life," he said, searching her gaze. "The safety of a prison, or the terrible joy that comes with freedom."

She stared up at him, stricken. He seemed to know the secret desires and fears of her innermost heart.

As if in slow motion, he lowered his mouth to hers, whispering, "Live dangerously."

She closed her eyes.

His kiss was electric, like sensual fire. She felt the smooth hot satin of his lips, felt the roughness of his chin, the powerful strength of his arms around her. The heat of his tongue was like liquid silk softly stroking inside her mouth. Sparks of pleasure spiraled down her body, making her breasts taut and heavy, tightening a coil of tension low and deep in her belly. Her nerve endings sizzled from her fingertips to her toes.

She felt as if she were exploding into pure light.

When he pulled away, she heard the low, hoarse gasp of his breath—or was it her own?

She stared up at him, knowing she'd remember that first kiss until the day she died.

Streaks of light moved across their skin as the limousine traveled through the city. They stared at each other, and Lilley's cheeks burned like the rest of her. She'd never known a dream could feel so real. So warm. So hot. She felt as if she were floating—flying. She blinked, feeling dizzy. She could almost see a trail of scattered diamonds sparkling against her skin where he'd touched her, like synesthesia.

Prince Alessandro Caetani could have had any woman he wanted. And he wanted *her*. He moved towards her, gently pushing her back against the leather seat, and she felt the hard weight of his body over her own. She felt his hands on her skin, and suddenly, she no longer felt like a timid, cowardly mouse.

She felt beautiful.

Powerful.

Reckless.

In his arms, she wasn't afraid. Of anything.

She closed her eyes, tossing back her head as he kissed down her throat with his hot, sensual mouth. "No one's ever made me feel like this," she breathed. "Touched me like this."

"I..." Suddenly his hands stilled against her skin. His head lifted. "But you've had other lovers," he said. "At least two."

Her eyes opened. She swallowed. "Not...exactly."

"How many have you had?"

"Technically, well...none."

He sat up, looking at her with wide, shocked eyes. "Are you trying to tell me you're a *virgin?*"

She sat up beside him, her mouth suddenly dry. "Is that a problem?"

He glared at her, his jaw hard. Turning, he pressed the button to lower the privacy shield.

"Sir?" the driver said courteously, not turning his head.

"Change of plans," Alessandro said. "We're taking Miss Smith home."

"What?" Lilley gasped. Her cheeks burned. "Why? That..." she glanced uneasily at the driver in the front seat, "that thing I just told you doesn't matter!"

Alessandro turned to Lilley with cold eyes. "Give Abbott your address."

Folding her arms, Lilley muttered out the address of her apartment building. The driver nodded and smoothly turned left at the next streetlight. Lilley waited for Alessandro to roll the limo's dividing window back up so they could have privacy. But he didn't, and she realized he intended to leave it open, keeping the driver as their de facto chaperone.

Setting her jaw, Lilley turned to stare out the window at the passing lights of the city. Her body felt suddenly cold. She felt bereft. Alone.

As they drove into the increasing traffic of the city, Alessandro wouldn't even look at her. Sulkily, Lilley picked up a plate of food. The dinner was delicious, but cold, and epicurean pleasures suddenly seemed small. The plate was empty by the time they reached her working-class neighborhood, when she realized that Alessandro really, truly did not intend to kiss her again.

Kiss her? He wasn't even going to *look* at her. Her night of magic, her time of feeling reckless and beautiful, was definitely over. But she couldn't accept it. After the brief, explosive joy she'd experienced so briefly in his arms, she couldn't just shrug off her loss and go quietly back to her empty apartment!

Her heart hammered in her throat. "You're making a fuss over nothing. It's not a big deal."

Alessandro looked at her. The lights and shadows of the city swept over the hard, angular lines of his cheekbones and jaw. "It is to me."

Glancing uneasily at the driver, she leaned towards Alessandro. "Just because I am slightly less experienced than your other lovers—"

"Do you not understand what I was offering?" he bit out. "A night. Perhaps two. Nothing more!"

"I wasn't asking for more!" she said, affronted.

"I will never go home to meet your parents, Lilley. I will not marry you." His dark eyes were furious. "I will not *love* you."

A pang went through her at his cold words, but she lifted her chin in defiance. "Who said I wanted love?"

"Virgins always do." He looked her up and down. "Do not be stupid, Lilley."

Stupid. Her cheeks felt suddenly cold as echoes of childhood taunts from school went through her. *Fri-lly, Li-lley, stupid and si-lly!*

Alessandro stared out the window, his jaw like stone. His body language informed her that he was done talking, his decision made.

The limo pulled to a stop at her building. The driver got out and opened her door. The night air rushed in, cool and clammy against her burning skin.

"Good night," Alessandro said coldly, not turning his head.

"This is really how you're going to end our date?" she whispered. "Kissing me—then kicking me to the curb?"

He turned, and his black eyes glowed like dying embers as a hard smile lifted his lips. "Now, *cara,* at last you understand what it means to be my lover."

Lilley stared at him. "I understand, all right," she choked out. Tears filled her eyes as she turned away. "You don't want me."

"Not want you?" he demanded.

She looked back, miserable and bewildered. "Yes, you just said—"

"I am saving you from a mistake," he said harshly. "Be grateful."

She swallowed. "Okay," she said. "Good-bye."

She stepped out onto the curb in front of her 1960s-era apartment building. She took a deep breath of the cool night air and looked down her dark, empty street, littered with parked cars. An old newspaper blew down the black asphalt like a tumbleweed. She'd only lived here two months, but she'd been in this same place for far too long. In France. In Minnesota.

Her apartment building towered over her, seeming almost malevolent in the darkness. She knew what waited for her there, too. Nadia would be out dancing with Jeremy all night, and Lilley would be alone. She'd curl up on the couch beneath her mother's old handmade quilt and watch television shows about other people's lives. Maybe she'd take a long bath, then lights out.

Was that doomed to be her whole life's fate?

She would never have left her cushy job as a housekeeper in France if her cousin hadn't been mean to the mother of his child, causing Lilley to quit her job in solidarity in an instinctive, emotional reaction that would have made her mother proud. But that had been the end of Lilley's courage. From the instant she'd set foot in San Francisco, she'd done nothing but hide.

We all must choose in this life, Alessandro had said. *The safety of a prison. Or the terrible joy that comes with freedom.*

"Lilley." His voice was hoarse in the limo behind her. "Damn you. Just go."

With an intake of breath, she turned back to face him. Without a word, without letting herself think, she climbed back into the limo. She felt his shocked stare, heard his intake of breath as she slammed the door behind her.

"Do you know the choice you're making?" he demanded harshly.

Her body trembled as she looked at him. "I used to dream of my first lover," she whispered. "I dreamed of a knight in shining armor who would adore me forever."

"And now?" he bit out.

"I'm just tired of being afraid." She swallowed, blinking back tears. "Tired of hiding from my own life."

He stared at her for a long moment. Then, pressing the

button to close the divider, he spoke a single word to the driver. “Sonoma.”

Lilley watched the divider lift higher, higher. It finally closed with a thunk, the noise reverberating like a door slamming behind her.

Then Alessandro moved. She had a single image of the dark heat of his eyes, the curve of his cruel, sensual mouth, as he pushed her back against the leather seat. Then his powerful body covered hers in a rough, ruthless embrace. His lips seared hers in a hot, hard kiss of sweetly poisonous honey.

Opening her mouth to his plunging tongue, she gave him—everything.

CHAPTER FOUR

AN HOUR later, as Alessandro carried her from the limo, Lilley blinked up at him in the moonlight, feeling drunk on his kisses. She felt hot, so hot. As he held her against his chest, she swayed with every step. The night was clear and the moon glowed in the velvet-black sky.

His Spanish-style villa was surrounded by rolling vineyards frosted with silvery light. In the distance, she could hear night birds calling.

The drive from the city had passed in seconds, it seemed, drenched with kisses. When the limo had arrived at the villa, she'd been so light-headed and breathless that she'd opened the door and fallen into a sprawl on the gravel driveway. Alessandro had picked her up in his strong arms, his gaze full of heat for what was to come.

Now, as the limo disappeared down the driveway, Lilley looked up at him in wonder. The stars seemed to move over his dark head, twinkling magically in the night sky.

She felt intoxicated, and she'd had only a glass and a half of champagne at the ball. There could be no doubt what—*who*—was drugging her senses.

At the door, he held her with one arm and punched in a security code. Around the villa, she briefly saw a pool and tennis courts and vast vineyards beyond. Then he opened the door with his shoulder and carried her inside, kicking the heavy door closed behind him.

Inside, the villa was dark and silent as he carried her up the 1920s-era wrought-iron stairs. He didn't have to say a word. She saw the whole sensual world in his dark eyes.

Upstairs, he pushed open a door at the end of the hall. She saw an enormous bed lit by a flood of moonlight from the windows. Reverently, he put her down on it. She shivered beneath the pool of silvery light as, never looking away from her, Alessandro pulled off his tuxedo tie and jacket and dropped them to the floor. He kicked off his shoes then climbed into bed beside her.

His hands were everywhere as he kissed her swollen lips. His embrace deepened, became hungrier and harder as his mouth pressed against hers, so hot and wet. His tongue twined with her own, and his hands cupped her breasts over the thin fabric of her gown, causing a gasp at the back of her throat. He stroked down to her waist, caressing her bare, shaking arms. Finally, he cradled her face and kissed her again with deepening fervor. She kissed him back with all the reckless passion of twenty-three lonely years.

There is nothing but now, she thought, dazed. *Nothing but this.*

She gasped as his hands moved beneath the clinging fabric of her bodice to her naked breasts. Her nipples tightened to hard points, sharpening in exquisite pleasure as he squeezed each of them gently between his fingers. Suddenly, he yanked the dress down, causing the spaghetti straps to snap as the fabric surrendered.

He showed rough brutality to her dress. But he caressed her body as if she were a precious, fragile treasure. His lips were hot against her skin as he moved down, nibbling her chin, licking her throat. She gasped as his large hands covered her full, naked breasts, squeezing each nipple, holding up each as a delicacy for the pleasure of his mouth. When he lowered his head, she felt the moist heat of his breath against her nipple and gripped the white bedspread beneath her. She held her breath as his entire mouth enfolded her nipple, suckling gently, his tongue swirling against her tight, swollen peak. She inhaled in tiny, desperate gasps as his hot, wet mouth moved to suckle the other breast in turn.

His hand stroked up her bare leg, dragging up the hemline of her long dress. The heavy weight of his hard, muscular body pressed her down into the softness of the bed, and she felt his fingertips languidly explore up her bare calf to caress the hollow behind her knee. As he suckled her breast, his hand continued to move upwards.

Stroking her outer thigh.

Her inner thigh.

She gripped the mattress, holding her breath. Alessandro lifted his mouth from her wet, hard nipple. Straddling her, he slowly unbuttoned his shirt. He tossed his platinum and diamond cufflinks carelessly to the floor. Wearing only his black tuxedo trousers, he moved down, between her legs, and she had her first look at the hard ripples and shadows of his bare chest in the moonlight. She bit down hard on her lip to stifle a gasp. His shoulders were broad, his muscles strong and powerful as an athlete's. The edges of his flat nipples were dusted lightly with dark hair that made a trail down his taut, defined belly before disappearing beneath his waistband. There wasn't an inch of fat anywhere on his body. She could hardly comprehend so much masculine beauty; he was like a dark angel.

At the end of the bed, Alessandro slid the dress off her unresisting body. Looking down, she realized she'd lost her high heels. Where? She couldn't remember. In the limo? Outside the villa? On the stairs…? It was all a sensual blur, and she was lost, utterly lost in sensation.

He pulled off his trousers and silk boxers, and Lilley's lips parted as she got a full look at the first wholly naked man she'd ever seen. And what a man. Her eyes traced over his powerful thighs, the strength of his body. And in the middle. She swallowed as her own breath suddenly choked her. Alessandro was huge. He would never fit inside her. Would he? Could he? How? Someone had made a mistake!

His dark eyes glowed in the shadows as he approached. She felt hypnotized, unable to move, unable even to cover her naked breasts or her lacy panties with her hands. He lay down beside her, turning her body to face him, and ran two fingertips down her side, from her shoulder to the swell of her breast to the valley of her waist and curve of her hip. She trembled, overwhelmed, helpless with desire.

Taking her hand, he gently suckled two of her fingers. Pulling her fingers from his mouth, he held her hand against his naked chest, looking at her. He seemed to be waiting. For what? What could he want…what could he expect from her…?

Taking her courage in her hands, shivering with her own daring, she leaned up and kissed him. His lips were hot and hard against hers, and as he let her set the rhythm, her confidence grew. A sigh of pleasure escaped her as he pushed her back against the soft pillows with a low growl, and covered her body with his own.

He was naked on top of her. Only the thin cotton of her panties separated them. She felt his hardness strain between her thighs, and the ache low in her belly increased. Closing her eyes, she gripped his shoulders as he kissed her, pulling him down harder.

Her head fell back with abandon as he kissed down her throat, kissing the valley between her breasts to the soft curve of her belly. She felt the swift flick of his tongue inside her belly button, but before she could be shocked, his teeth were gently pulling down the top edge of her panties.

He pushed her legs apart and she felt his breath against her thighs. She shivered as he kissed up her legs. He gave a teasing lick beneath the bottom edge of her panties, and her fingernails gripped into his shoulders. She held her breath, eyes still squeezed shut, as his hand cupped the mound between her legs. He sucked her most sensitive spot through the lacy fabric, and she cried out.

He ripped off her panties, tossing them on the floor in a mangled heap of lace. Her eyes flew open and she took a single deep gulp of air before she felt his mouth on her. Right on her. Licking her, spreading her wide with his fingers so he could taste every slick fold. She felt wet, so wet. His tongue played with her, teasing her, one moment lapping her with its full width, then moving to flick her sensitive nub with the tip. The feeling of his mouth on her was like nothing she'd imagined, pleasure so intense it was almost agony. She was being sucked into a maelstrom of ecstasy, drowning in the waves. Her hips lifted of their own accord to meet his mouth as the tension in her deepest core built higher and higher.

She couldn't endure this sweet torture, this agony of pleasure, for much longer. She writhed beneath him, her body twisting as she tried to pull away from the insistent, ruthless pleasure of his tongue. But he held her hips firmly, spreading her wider still, as he suckled between her legs. He thrust one thick finger inside her to the first knuckle. Then two fingers. Then three, going deeper, stretching her wide, giving her a small shock of pain to season and salt the sweet, wide, wet slide of his tongue.

Her body arched off the bed as she tried to move away from his fingers inside her, but he would not let her escape the exquisite agony of her pleasure. She gripped the bedspread as the storm inside her exploded. As if from a distance, she heard the cry from her lips lift to a scream of joy.

Sheathing himself in a condom, Alessandro lifted his powerful body over hers, as she still arched in ecstasy on the bed. Positioning himself, he whispered in her ear, "I'm sorry."

He pushed inside her in a single stroke, shoving himself to the hilt. The sudden pain made her gasp. As he filled her so deeply, ripping the invisible barrier inside her, Lilley's scream of joy changed to a choked gasp. He held perfectly still, letting her get used to the stretch of him inside her.

"I'm sorry," he murmured again. Lowering his head, he kissed her face, her cheeks, her lips. "The only way over it is through it." Her answer was a muffled sob as she turned her face into the pillow.

Then slowly, very slowly, he began to move inside her, and a miracle happened. The ocean of pleasure, which had receded beneath her like a wave, sucking sand beneath her feet, began to rush in like the tide. Having him inside her started to feel…good. She'd thought she was satiated, but to her shock a new need built within her. With each slow, deep thrust, he filled a place deep inside her that made her body tighten with new desire.

As her body accepted him fully, Alessandro moved with increasing roughness, riding her harder and deeper, holding her hips with his hands. Her breasts swayed with the increasing force of his thrusts, the headboard slapping against the wall. The pleasure—the pain—made her writhe, her back arching off the bed as she panted for breath, her body desperate with the need for new release. He held her down as he pushed inside her, and he was so huge, so deep, and it felt good, so good. She held her breath, closing her eyes. Her head tilted back and the tension inside her coiled—and coiled—then sprang.

She gave a silent, mindless scream as explosions ripped through her, shaking her whole body as at, the same moment, she heard his growl rise to a shout and he slammed into her with one final, cataclysmic thrust.

When Lilley opened her eyes, she found Alessandro lying on top of her, holding her protectively. She closed her eyes. For no reason she could explain, she suddenly felt like crying. Except he'd taken her to a whole new world.

Why had she ever been so afraid of something so magical?

"I hurt you. I'm sorry."

At the sound of his low voice, she looked up at his face. The shadowed mystery of his dark eyes held regret and barely satiated desire and something more.

"You didn't," she lied.

He gave her a skeptical look.

"A little," she admitted, then, tossing her arms above her head against the soft pillow, she sighed happily. "But would it be cheesy to say it hurt so good?"

He tenderly kissed her forehead. "Horribly cheesy."

Then he kissed her mouth with something more than tenderness. His kiss deepened, his tongue twining with her own as his hands cupped her cheeks. She sighed with pleasure, then gave an involuntary wince as he crushed her bruised lips.

"I'm hurting you." He started to roll over, but she stopped him.

"You're not."

"You're lying."

"So let me," she whispered.

A sensual smile curved his lips. He kissed her again, his mouth hot and hard against hers. She felt him move against her, and sighed with bliss.

He suddenly rolled her over on the bed, pulling her on

top of his naked body. She gave a little squeak of surprise as he looked up at her with dark, wicked eyes. "Your turn."

Lilley stared at him. He expected her to lead in bed? To ride him? Her heart pounded in her throat. She was so clumsy. She'd make a fool of herself. "I…I don't think I can do this. I don't know how."

"You will." Looking straight into her eyes, he put his hand on her cheek. "I can teach you."

Alessandro leaned up to kiss her, and she forgot to be afraid. Holding on to him, letting him guide her to find her own rhythm, she allowed him to teach her to follow her own pleasure, and lead him to his. She rode him, and joy and freedom filled her soul. For the first time in her life, Lilley was the fearless woman she'd always wanted to be.

Alessandro had never known sex could be like this. Lilley was an intoxicating combination of innocence and fire.

He'd never been so insatiable before. He knew that for the rest of his life he'd remember how he'd had the honor of being her first lover. He'd remember teaching her to control the rhythm and pace as she rode him, timidly at first, then with rising reckless confidence.

Afterward, sweaty and sticky from lovemaking, they'd showered in the enormous, gleaming marble bathroom. Alessandro had watched her as she'd tipped her head back beneath the water. The sight of her arching body as water poured over her breasts and streamed off her tight, pink nipples had been too much for him. She'd flicked him a teasing glance, and he'd suddenly realized she was playing with him. With a growl, he'd pushed her against the cool marble of the shower and made love to her against the wall as hot water sprayed all over them both.

Lilley was a very apt student. No wonder each sexual encounter between them was more explosive than the last.

His innocent virgin was transforming into a wanton sex goddess in front of his eyes.

Rosy-skinned and exhausted, they'd fallen into bed a few hours before dawn and woken up starving a few hours later. They'd made love a fourth time, fast and hot, then ventured downstairs for breakfast.

Alessandro found himself wanting to impress her. He'd given his staff the weekend off, so he made her his signature breakfast dish, a sausage frittata. As he cooked, she scooted around the kitchen wearing an oversized robe, gathering ingredients for her French toast, a delicious confection of nutmeg and cinnamon sugar. They sat together at his kitchen table, basking in the morning light, drinking freshly squeezed orange juice and feeding each other bites of food.

For the first time in Alessandro's adult life, he had no desire to check in with work, or catch up on the morning news. All he wanted to do was look at her, touch her, be with her. He couldn't get enough of her exquisite skin and her curvaceous, soft body.

But it was more than just her body.

Being around Lilley made him feel…different. Made him *feel* his own heart beating. After so many years of being empty and bored, playing the game, making money to keep score, sleeping with women he barely knew and dodging the constant onslaught of people begging for his attention, he could let down his guard. Lilley asked for nothing. She would never hurt him or lie to him. Her openness and honesty reminded him of the person he'd been long ago, before everyone he loved had betrayed him.

For some reason, Lilley liked him. Not his money or his title or even just his body. She liked *him*. The man inside. And looking at her in the morning light, Alessandro realized that whatever he'd promised her yesterday, he had no intention of giving her up. He didn't care if it was selfish.

He wanted more than a one-night stand.

"This is delicious," Lilley murmured, leaning forward at the breakfast table. Her oversized robe fell open to reveal her delectable breasts as she took another bite of frittata. She gave him an impish smile. "To be honest, I didn't expect cooking to be one of your talents."

A moment before, he'd been finishing his last piece of French toast, licking the crumbs off his plate. But looking at her state of undress instantly made him want her again, made him want to sweep their dishes to the floor and make love to her on the table. He swallowed. "I usually don't cook. You inspired me."

She smiled at him, her trusting warm eyes the color of deep, dark caramel, her beautiful face suffused in the soft glow of morning light as she whispered, "Not half as much as you inspire me."

Alessandro stared at her, lost in her gaze. He could no more stop himself from wanting her than he could stop breathing.

But keeping her would be wrong. Very wrong.

I have no reason to feel guilty, he told himself fiercely. He'd tried to let her go once already. She'd made her own choice. He'd told her up front he could never marry her or love her. She could protect her own heart.

Reaching his hand out to her cheek, he slowly stroked down her neck to her swelling breasts half revealed by the gape of her robe. Her lips parted in surprise and he could not resist the invitation. Leaning over the table, he kissed her. He felt her soft lips move against his, matching his passion, and nearly groaned. Selfish or not, nothing on earth could make him give her up. Not now. Not yet.

Rising to his feet, Alessandro pulled her from her chair.

Untying her sash, he dropped her robe to the floor, leaving her naked skin glowing in a pool of morning light. He gave a shuddering intake of breath. "Walk ahead of me," he said hoarsely. "So I can see you."

Her eyebrow quirked. In a quick movement, she jerked open his own robe, dropping it to the floor beside hers.

"You first," she suggested sweetly.

Thirty seconds later, Lilley was giggling with little screams of laughter as he chased her, both of them naked, back upstairs. They didn't even make it to his bedroom, but ended up on the priceless heirloom rug in the upstairs hall.

They spent the rest of Sunday making love in every room of his villa. In the garden, in the library, in the study, and finally, long past midnight, back in his bed. They fell asleep wrapped in each other's arms.

But now, just a few hours before Monday's dawn, Alessandro was wide awake as Lilley slept beside him. He'd lost count of the number of times they'd made love in the last thirty hours. More than ten. He paused, then shook his head, amazed. Less than twenty?

Each time he possessed her, instead of being satiated, he only wanted her more. His passion for her consumed him, and his hunger only grew.

But their weekend was over. He looked down at her, kissing her forehead softly as she slept in his arms. He listened to her breath. She clung to him, naked, sighing sweetly in her sleep as she whispered something that sounded like his name.

Guilt, a very unfamiliar emotion, blew through Alessandro like an icy breeze. Virgins fell in love. He knew that too well. They were not experienced enough in the ways of the world to separate their bodies from their hearts. And a girl like Lilley, so warm, vivid, brilliant and kind, deserved a man who could give her a future. A man who could actually love her.

Unlike his usual sort of mistress, Lilley Smith was not a ruthless coquette who used her body as a weapon for power and gain. He wondered if he could ever again be fully satisfied by a cold-hearted woman like Olivia Bianchi. How could that ever compare to Lilley's intoxicating warmth and joy as she gave all of herself, body and soul?

Already Alessandro wanted her again.

Angrily, he clawed back his hair, which was still damp from the sweat of their passionate night. Careful not to wake her, he rose to his feet and walked naked through the balcony doors, out into the warm, clear August night. Moonlight stretched over his vineyards, frosting the hills with silver as he looked out at his land, trying to calm his unquiet heart.

He closed his eyes, feeling every bit of his thirty-five years. His soul felt old and dark compared to hers. Was that his intention—to suck up her youth and optimism like a vampire, feeding on her innocence until his own darkness consumed her?

"Alessandro?" he heard her murmur sleepily.

Gripping his hands, he went back into the bedroom. He found her lying in bed, her gorgeous curves covered only by a sheet. She sat up in surprise when she realized he'd been standing naked on the balcony. "What's wrong?"

"Nothing," he said.

She swallowed, biting her lip. "Do you regret our time together?" she whispered. "Are you thinking about—Olivia?"

"No!" Shaking his head, he said the first thing that came to mind. "I'm thinking about the Mexico City deal. Wondering how our design team in San Francisco will update the Joyería designs once they take over."

Alessandro closed his mouth with a snap, shocked at his

own stupidity. He'd been so concerned about not hurting Lilley, he'd blurted out something he should never have revealed to anyone except his board of directors. If it became public, it would ruin everything. He'd given Joyería's current owner, Miguel Rodriguez, some legally vague reassurances that he would keep the Mexican designers on staff and the studio in Mexico City separate from Caetani Worldwide's offices in San Francisco, Shanghai and Rome. If Rodriguez heard about his plans to economize, the man could well cancel the deal and sell the company to a competitor.

Alessandro looked at Lilley sharply, but she seemed completely unaware of the import of the information he'd unthinkingly shared. She smiled, shaking her head.

"You always work, don't you?" she said softly. "That's why you're so successful." Her gaze grew troubled as she hugged a pillow over her breasts. "Maybe if I were more like you, I wouldn't be such a screw-up."

He frowned. "A screw-up?" he demanded. "Who said that?"

Her smile became sad. "No one has to say it. I came to San Francisco to start my jewelry business, then chickened out." She looked down at the bed. "I'm not brave like you."

He sat down beside her. "There are all kinds of bravery in the world, *cara.*" Reaching over, he lifted her chin, forcing her to meet his gaze. "You have an open heart. You trust people in a way I could not. And your jewelry is unique and beautiful. Like you," he said huskily. Setting his jaw, he gave her a decisive nod. "You will start your business when the time is right. I know it."

Her large brown eyes looked up at him with almost painful hope. "You do?"

"Yes." He dropped his hand. "I failed many times, in

many different businesses, before I made my first fortune. Selling children's plastic bracelets, of all things."

She gave an amazed laugh. "You? Selling plastic bracelets? I don't believe it."

He gave her a sudden grin. "It's true. The trend exploded across America and I made my first million. I was determined to succeed. No matter how many times I failed, I wouldn't give up." He stroked her hair. "You are the same. You just don't know it yet."

"You think so?" she breathed, her eyes huge.

He nodded. "If it's important to you, you'll make it happen. Whatever it costs."

"What made you so driven to succeed?"

His lips flattened. "When my father died, he left debts I had to repay. I dropped out of college and worked twenty hours a day." He looked away. "I will never feel powerless again."

"Powerless? But you're a prince!"

"Prince of nothing," he said harshly. "An empty title I inherited from a fifteenth-century warlord. The men of my family have always been corrupt and weak."

"But not you." Her clear eyes met his. "You are the leader of Caetani Worldwide. You built a billion-dollar company from nothing. Everyone loves you," she whispered.

He felt uncomfortable with the adoration he saw in her eyes. "I'm nothing special," he said gruffly. "If I can start a business, so can you. Start a business plan, work through the numbers."

"That might be hard, since I read letters and numbers in the wrong order."

"Dyslexia?"

She nodded.

"What is it like?"

"It's different for different people. In my case the letters and numbers won't stay put."

He barked a laugh. "And you're working in my file room?"

She gave him a sudden cheeky grin. "Now you understand why I was working late." Her voice became wistful. "I've never been really successful at anything except making jewelry. Maybe that's why my father thinks I'm hopeless at taking care of myself. He threatened to disinherit me if I don't come back to Minnesota and marry one of his managers."

"Disinherit you!" Alessandro pictured a hard-working farmer with a small plot of land in the bleak northern plains. "He wanted you to marry a manager on his farm?"

Lilley blinked, frowning at him. "My father's not a farmer. He's a businessman."

"Ah," Alessandro said. "He owns a restaurant? Perhaps a laundromat?"

Her eyes slid away evasively. "Um. Something like that. My parents got divorced a few years ago, when my mother was sick. The day she died was the worst day of my life. I had to get away, so I found…a job…with a distant relative. My cousin."

She stumbled strangely over the words, looking at him with an anxiety he couldn't understand.

"I'm sorry," Alessandro said in a low voice. "My mother died a few years ago, and my own relationship with my father was always complicated." *Complicated* was an understatement. His father, Prince Luca Caetani, had married Alessandro's mother for her money, then spent it on his mistresses. He'd died when Alessandro was nineteen, leaving debts and an unknown number of bastards around the world. Alessandro was his father's only legitimate child, the heir to the Caetani title and name, but every year some stranger came out of the woodwork, claiming blood ties and asking for a handout from the company Alessandro had built with his own two hands.

Just wait till you're older, son, his father had gasped on his deathbed. *You'll be just like me. You'll see.*

Alessandro had vowed he would never be anything like his father. He was selfish, but not a monster.

Right?

"I actually thought about going back." Lilley's trusting eyes shone at him. "But now I know I won't. You make me feel…brave. Like I can do anything. Risk anything."

Alessandro's heart gave a sickening lurch. He gripped his fists so tightly the knuckles turned white.

Lilley was half in love with him already. He could see it in her face, even if she herself wasn't aware of it yet. If he kept her as his mistress, how long would it be before he obliterated her light completely? Until she, too, had a heart as dark and empty as night?

He'd crossed a line. He'd violated her innocence in a way he could never take back.

If that wasn't the work of a monster, what was?

With an intake of breath, he turned away. In just an hour or two, dawn would break across the purple hills. But there could be no sunrise for Alessandro. He felt cold to the bone.

There was only one way to cut her loss. One way to leave her heart bruised, but not shattered. He exhaled, closing his eyes.

He had to let her go.

"It's almost morning," she said, sounding sad. She splayed her small hand against his chest. "In a few hours, I'll go back to the file room. What about you?"

He opened his eyes. "Mexico City."

Lilley took a deep breath. "Alessandro," she whispered, "I want you to know that I—"

Turning to her almost violently, he put his finger against her lips. "Let's not talk." Pulling her down on the mattress beside him, he breathed in the scent of her, the intoxicating smell of sunshine and flowers. He gloried in her warmth and beauty for the last time.

"This has been the happiest day of my life," she whispered. "I'm just sad to see it end." She gave him a crooked smile. "In a few hours, you'll forget I ever existed."

He looked down at her. "I'll never forget you, Lilley," he said, and it was the truth.

"Oh," she breathed. Relief and gratitude filled her eyes. She thought his words meant they might have a future. She didn't know they were the death knell for any relationship they might have had.

She put her hand on his rough, unshaven cheek. "Then give me a kiss I'll never forget."

He looked at her full, rosy lips, and his whole body shuddered with need.

One last time, he told his conscience savagely. He would give her up at dawn. Set her free before he did any further damage to her soul.

Cupping her face, Alessandro kissed her, as if trying to burn the memory of her lips against his for all time. Tasting the sweetness of her mouth, he spread her lips wide, plundering her with his tongue. Pulling the pillow away from her body, he rolled her beneath him on the bed, covering her naked body with his own.

Alessandro looked down at Lilley's beautiful face. He knew the bitter memory of the joy shining now in her sweet, joyful eyes, her strange trust and belief in his goodness would haunt him for all time. An ache like regret pierced his soul.

Then, closing his eyes, he pushed himself inside her.

CHAPTER FIVE

A MONTH later, Lilley felt sick as she sat in a hard office chair in the basement office of the human resources department. The fluorescent lights above the desk flickered and hummed as Lilley licked her dry lips, praying she'd heard wrong.

"What?" she croaked.

"I'm sorry, Miss Smith, but we must let you go." The kindly older man on the other side of the desk shifted uncomfortably in his chair. "I'm afraid Caetani Worldwide isn't the right place for your skills."

Fighting nausea, Lilley took a deep breath as grief and pain washed over her. She'd known this would happen, known she'd lose her job no matter how hard she tried. Effort couldn't compensate for her slowness in filing numbers and letters that danced in front of her eyes.

Maybe she really was incapable of taking care of herself, just as her father said. Case in point: she'd slept with her boss, and then was surprised when Alessandro disappeared before she woke up on Monday morning and never bothered to contact her again. Exactly as he'd told her he'd do. Her throat suddenly hurt. She really wasn't smart.

"I can assure you," the HR director continued, "there's a very generous compensation package."

"I was too slow, right?" she whispered, blinking back tears. "I took too long to finish my work."

The man shook his head, his ponderous jowls wobbling. He didn't look as if he wanted to fire her. He looked as if he wished the earth would swallow him up beneath his desk. "You did a good job, Miss Smith. You were popular with the rest of the staff. Yes, you took longer than the other file clerk, but your work ethic—" He took a deep breath, tapping a file on his desk. "That's neither here nor there." His voice was clipped. "We will give you an excellent recommendation and I can assure you that you'll find a job soon. Very, *very* soon."

He started to explain the details of her severance package, but Lilley barely listened. The sick feeling was starting to win, so she focused on her breathing, staring hard at the little gray trash can on the floor by his desk. Fighting the desire to throw up into it.

"I'm sorry it turned out this way," he said finally. "But someday you'll be glad that..." He saw that she wasn't listening and was clutching her stomach with one hand while covering her mouth with her other. He sighed. "Please sign this." He pushed a paper towards her on the desk. Grabbing the pen he offered, Lilley skimmed the document—her father had drummed that much into her, at any rate—and saw she was basically promising not to sue the company for sexual harassment. Harassment?

She sucked in her breath. That meant it wasn't her work that was at fault, but she was being fired by—

She cut off the thought, unable to bear his name. Scribbling her signature, she rose to her feet. The HR director shook her hand.

"Best of luck, Miss Smith."

"Thanks," she choked out. Grabbing the file he held out,

she fled to the women's bathroom, where she could be sick in privacy.

Afterward, Lilley splashed cold water on her face. She looked at her wan, green expression in the mirror. She tried to force a grin, to put the cheerful mask back in place that she'd worn for the last month while enduring teasing and innuendo about Prince Alessandro. But today, she couldn't even smile.

Fired. She was fired.

Numbly, she walked to the elevator. She exited on the third floor and went to her desk in the corner of the windowless file room. Other employees had pictures of family or friends or pets hanging at their desks. Lilley had a lonely pink geranium and a postcard that her cousin's wife, Carrie, had sent from Provence a few weeks ago. On the tidy surface of her desk, she saw someone had left a gossip magazine for her to find. Again.

Her body felt cold as she looked down at the latest issue of *Celebrity Weekly.* The cover had a picture of Alessandro in Mexico City, where he'd been living for the last month in his attempt to keep the Joyería deal from falling apart. But last week, Lilley's cousin Théo had made a successful counterbid. It should have made her feel glad, but it didn't. Her heart ached to think of how Alessandro would feel after failing—at anything.

At least she was used to it.

Her eyes moved to a smaller picture at the bottom of the magazine's cover that had been taken at the Cannes film festival months before. Alessandro wore a tuxedo, looking darkly handsome, holding the hand of a beautiful blonde dressed in black. Olivia Bianchi.

Playboy Prince to Wed at Last, the cover blared. Someone had underlined the words with a thick black pen.

Ever since she'd been Alessandro's date at the ball, she'd

been paying for it. Some of her coworkers had worried Lilley might think too well of herself for briefly being their boss's mistress. Well, she thought bitterly, no chance of that.

Lilley jumped as she heard a man clear his throat behind her. Turning, she saw Larry, a security guard she knew. Just yesterday, Lilley had given him advice about how to get ink stains out of fabric, something she'd dealt with fairly often as her cousin's housekeeper. But today, his face was regretful and resigned.

"Sorry, Lilley. I'm supposed to escort you out."

She nodded over the lump in her throat. She gathered up her geranium, the magazine, the postcard from Provence, her nubby old cardigan and the large bag of toffees she kept at the bottom of her desk for emergencies. She packed up her life in a cardboard box and followed the security guard from the file room, trying to ignore all the employees staring at her as she was escorted from the building in a walk of shame.

In the lobby, Larry checked her cardboard box for contraband—what did he think she might take? Pens? Copy paper?—and then took her employee pass card. "Sorry," he mumbled again.

"I'll be fine," she whispered, and was proud she managed to leave the building without either crying or throwing up.

Numbly, Lilley took the bus home. As she reached her apartment, her cell phone rang. She glanced at the number. Nadia had missed all the action, so Jeremy must have told her the news. But Lilley couldn't face her roommate's sympathy right now. Or the suspicions Nadia had voiced lately, which Lilley was desperately trying not to think about: the reason for her frequent nausea over the last week.

Turning her phone to Mute, she threw it on the counter. She gulped down some dry crackers and water to help her stomach calm down, then changed into flannel pajamas and a pink fleece robe. Wrapping herself in her mother's quilt, she lay down on the couch and closed her eyes, even though she knew she was far too upset to sleep.

She was woken by the rattle of her cell phone on the kitchen counter. Sitting up, she saw the deepening shadows and realized she'd slept for hours. Pulling a pillow over her head, she tried to ignore the rattle. The phone finally stopped buzzing, then after a brief pause, it rudely started again. Muttering to herself, Lilley got up and grabbed it. She blinked when she saw the out-of-state number. *Alessandro,* she thought, still half confused by her dream, the dream she'd had over and over all month. She could still feel the heat of his lips against her skin. She swallowed.

"Hello?" she said almost timidly.

"Lilley Smith?" a jovial voice boomed at the other end. "You don't know me, but your résumé has come to our attention, and we'd like to offer you a paid internship with our company in New York."

By the time Lilley hung up the phone, her dreams about Alessandro were gone. She finally understood. He wasn't just ridding her from his company. He was completely erasing her from his life.

Her eyes fell on the magazine, visible from the cardboard box on the kitchen counter. Snatching it up, she stared with narrowed eyes at the picture of Alessandro with Olivia Bianchi. The blond Italian socialite looked like a smug, satisfied Persian cat who'd just licked up a whole bowl of cream.

Another huge wave of nausea overwhelmed her. Tossing the magazine to the floor, she covered her mouth and ran down the hall. Afterward, her eyes fell on the brown paper bag that sat ominously on the sink, like a loaded gun. Nadia had bought it for her days ago at the drugstore, and Lilley had scrupulously ignored it.

She couldn't possibly be pregnant. They'd gone through boxes of condoms! They'd used protection *every single time,* all weekend long.

Except...

She froze. Except that one time. In the shower.

Wide-eyed, she stared at herself in the bathroom mirror.

She exhaled. How could their affair have ended so badly? She'd fallen asleep so happily in Alessandro's arms, foolishly believing they might have a future. Then she'd woken up alone. Wrapping herself in a bedsheet, she'd called his name teasingly as she went downstairs. Instead, she'd discovered only his housekeeper. "The prince has been called away," the woman said stiffly. "Abbott will drive you back to the city." She'd handed Lilley the red gown, mended and pressed, and served her eggs, coffee and toast at the same table where Lilley had enjoyed that joyful, sensual breakfast with Alessandro just the day before. The chauffeur had driven her back home without a word. Lilley's cheeks still burned to remember.

But in spite of everything, she couldn't regret their time together. How could she, when she'd finally discovered what it felt like to take risks? To be truly alive? She'd discovered passion that had been like a fire consuming her body, making her soul blaze like a beacon in the night.

All right, so she'd never see him again. She could accept that, since she had no choice. She could even be grateful for the experience. For the memory.

But what if she was pregnant?

Lilley squeezed her eyes shut, her heart pounding. She would take the test and find out for sure. It would prove once and for all that she'd just eaten some bad Chinese takeout or something.

Her hands shook as she took the test, then waited. She told herself she wasn't worried. Hummed a cheerful little lullaby she'd sung to her cousin's baby in France. Looked at her watch. Two minutes. It was probably too soon to check, but it wouldn't hurt just to—

Pregnant.

Pregnantpregnantpregnant.

Her shaking hands dropped the stick in the trash as she staggered down the hall and into the kitchen. She found herself with a kettle in her hand and realized she was making tea, just as her mother had always done in times of crisis.

"Sweetheart, there are very few problems in the world that can't be made better by a hug, a plate of cookies and a cup of tea," her mother had said, smiling. It had worked like a charm when Lilley was nine and had failed a spelling test, and when she was a teenager and the other kids mocked, "Guess your father can't buy you a new brain." It had even worked when her father had asked her sick mother for a divorce, abandoning their family home in Minneapolis to build a huge mansion for his mistress on the shores of Lake Minnetonka.

She swallowed, trembling as tears filled her eyes. The difference was that her mother had been there. Lilley missed her so much. Paula Smith would have hugged her daughter, told her everything was going to be all right. And Lilley would have believed her.

The kettle screamed. Numbly, Lilley poured boiling water over the fragrant peppermint tea. Holding her steaming, oversized mug in her shaking hands, Lilley went to the couch.

A baby.

She was going to have Alessandro's baby.

Raw, jagged emotion washed over her. He'd arranged for her to be fired and had offered a job that was three thousand miles away. There was no other explanation for her to be spontaneously head-hunted for a fantastic internship with a New York jewelry company at double her current salary. He wanted Lilley out of San Francisco, so he wouldn't have to see her *scurrying in the halls* and could settle down, mouse-free, with his beautiful, sleek bride.

Setting her mug on the end table, she picked up the magazine from the floor. Opening it, she skimmed through the article. Alessandro was holding his annual wine-harvest celebration at his villa in Sonoma. Rumor was that it was going to be an engagement party.

Friday. That was tonight.

Lilley's fingertips stroked the image of Alessandro's handsome, cold face. She'd been so sure he would want to see her again. For the last month, she'd jumped every time her cell phone rang. She'd had such naive faith. She'd expected him to call, send flowers, a card, *something.* He hadn't.

But it turned out he had given her something, the greatest gift any woman could receive. A baby. She placed her hand on her soft belly. She'd always disliked her plump figure, wishing she could be thin and athletic. But now she realized her extra pounds didn't matter. Her amazing body was creating a baby. How could she be anything but grateful to it?

How would Alessandro react when she told him?

The memory of his harsh voice came floating back to her. *I will not marry you. I will not love you.*

She'd known from the beginning that Alessandro only considered her a fling. He'd been honest from the start. If Lilley had a broken heart, she was the only one to blame, because she'd allowed herself to hope for more.

Setting down the magazine, Lilley rose to her feet and walked to the tiny window in her pink fleece robe. Opening the gingham curtains, she looked out into the quiet street, remembering the night she'd made the choice that had changed her life so completely, the night she'd decided to give her virginity to Alessandro.

She would regret leaving San Francisco. She'd come to love the city, and had even become friends again with Jeremy and Nadia. Perhaps she would come to appreciate New York. But she would be going alone.

Then she remembered: she'd never be alone again.

She placed her hand on her belly as a wave of joy, sudden and unexpected as a child's laugh, washed over her. How could she be sad about how her time with Alessandro had ended, when he'd given her such a gift?

And the grip around her heart loosened. She would leave, as he wanted. But there was one thing she had to do first. She couldn't exactly make an appointment to see him via Mrs. Rutherford, who was highly skilled at blocking former lovers from contacting him. And this wasn't the sort of news she wished to convey via his business email address. He'd deliberately never given her his private phone number. So as unpalatable as it was, that left only one option.

Picking up the magazine, she looked down at his hard, handsome face, and at the image of the villa in Sonoma where they'd first made love. Where he'd taken her virginity. Where he'd filled her with his child.

Before she left him forever, she had to tell Alessandro he was going to be a father.

"*Alessandro,* at last." Olivia's sultry voice immediately set Alessandro's nerves on edge. "Did you miss me, darling?"

Forcing his lips into a smile, Alessandro turned to face her, his shoulders tight. He'd seen her arrive through the window of his study. His first party guest to arrive tonight.

It was unlike Olivia to be early to anything, so that meant she'd heard the rumors. And unfortunately the rumors were true.

The five-carat diamond ring in his jacket pocket felt like an anchor, heavy enough to drag him down through the floors of his villa, through his wine cellar and continuing straight to hell.

"I've missed you." Olivia gave him a smile that showed her white teeth. She was impeccably dressed as always, in a black one-shoulder cocktail dress that showed off her tanned body, muscular and slender from hours of running and self-denial. As she came towards him, her diamond bangles jangled noisily on her skinny wrist. She'd be the perfect Caetani bride, he told himself firmly.

And he needed to settle down before he became every bit as reckless and corrupt as his father. His night with Lilley had shown that all too clearly.

Alessandro pushed away the memory of Lilley's big trusting eyes and soft, sensual body that always hovered on the edge of his consciousness. He never should have allowed himself to touch her. Never.

Olivia came forward to kiss his mouth, but at the last moment, his head twisted away, causing her lips to land squarely on his cheek. His body's abrupt reaction surprised them both. Surely his body, at least, should have been pleased to see her? He hadn't had sex for a month. And what a hellish month it had been.

She drew back, her eyes offended. "What is it?"

"Nothing." What could he say? That he'd missed her while he was in Mexico City? That he'd thought of her when he'd lost his bid on Joyería to his most hated rival, that French bastard Théo St. Raphaël?

The truth was that it hadn't been Olivia's face he'd yearned to see the night he'd suffered that bitter disappointment. He'd hungered for a different woman's face. Her soft body. Her kind heart.

Alessandro took a deep breath. Lilley was likely already packing for New York. She almost certainly hated him now. He could only imagine how she'd felt this past month since he'd abandoned her without even the bare courtesy of a farewell. Usually his one-night stands at least got flowers.

But his coldness was deliberate. He was being cruel to be kind.

Olivia's red lips lifted into a determined smile. "I was so glad when you called me," she murmured. "I was almost starting to think you'd broken up with me."

"I did." He stared down at her. "I do not care for ultimatums."

"Lesson learned," she said, still smiling, though it did not meet her eyes. She tucked her hand into his own. Her skin felt cool. She had no softness, either of body or soul. "I'm glad we're back together. We're perfect for each other, aren't we?"

Alessandro looked down at her beautiful face, her big green eyes and sharp, hollow cheekbones. Physically, she didn't have a single flaw. She would fit well into his world. No one would ever be able to hurt her or criticize her performance as his *principessa. "Sì,"* he said tightly. *"Perfetto."*

They walked down the hall towards the two-story foyer. From the landing, he saw many new guests had already arrived. This party had been planned in celebration of the early wine harvest, just for a few friends. But six weeks ago, feeling arrogantly certain of impending success with the Joyería deal, he'd invited business associates, thinking it would be the perfect victory lap.

Instead, the grape harvest was turning weak and the Mexico City deal was a failure. And he was going to propose to Olivia. It wasn't a celebration. It was a wake.

With every step, he felt the dead weight of the diamond ring grow heavier in his pocket. He wondered who'd leaked the story about him purchasing it in Mexico City. Some underpaid store clerk, most likely. He'd carried it for over a week now, but he'd called Olivia only two days ago.

He'd been dragging his heels, but now he'd made his decision and wouldn't go back. He was thirty-five and had defiled one virgin too many. He'd selfishly and ruthlessly possessed Lilley, when he'd known it would ultimately bring her pain. He'd sworn he'd never be like his selfish, callous father. And yet, seducing his innocent, brokenhearted file-room girl, he'd come perilously close.

Olivia's cool, bony arm twisted hard around his as they walked down the stairs. The weather forecast was calling for thunderstorms, so the party had been moved indoors from the pool, although many guests had remained outside. He could hear a jazz trio playing in the ballroom, and he saw friends and business acquaintances from Silicon Valley. The men wore suits similar to Alessandro's, and their wives wore shiny cocktail dresses, and everyone was drinking his wine. He should be enjoying this…shouldn't he?

He heard Bronson arguing loudly at the door. His normally staid butler seemed to be struggling with an unwanted guest. "Service entrance is at the back," Bronson insisted, trying to close the door.

"I'm not here for a delivery!" a woman said, pushing at the door. "I'm here to see Alessandro!"

The butler sucked in his breath as if she'd just insulted his mother. *"Alessandro?"* he repeated in disbelief. "You mean His Serene Highness, Prince Alessandro Caetani?"

"Yes!"

"The prince is currently hosting a party," Bronson said coldly, his tone clearly adding *and is unavailable to the likes of you.* "Make an appointment though his secretary. Good evening."

But as he started to slam the door, the woman blocked him with a foot. "I'm sorry to be rude," she begged, "but I'm leaving in the morning and have to see him. Tonight."

Prickles went down Alessandro's neck.

He knew that sweet voice. It was clear as a freshwater lake to a man dying of thirst. Dropping Olivia's hand, he went down the stairs to where white-haired, dignified Bronson was struggling with the door like an American bouncer at a bar. The butler panted, "Unhand the door this instant—"

Grabbing the door over his head, Alessandro wrenched it open. The butler turned. "Your highness," he gasped. "I'm sorry for this interruption. This *woman* has been trying to force her way into your party. I don't know how she talked her way past security at the gate, but..."

"It's all right," Alessandro said, hardly knowing what he was saying, staring at the woman from his dreams on the doorstep.

Lilley looked even more beautiful than she had a month ago. Her long brown hair was swept back in a ponytail, her face was bare of makeup. Unlike all the other women squeezed into tight girdles and barely able to move in sequined dresses, Lilley wore a simple tank top and a flowery cotton skirt, a casual summery outfit that effortlessly showed off her stunning curves. She shone like an angel standing in front of the distant dark storm clouds over the horizon.

"Alessandro," Lilley whispered, looking at him. The pupils of her large, limpid eyes seemed to dilate, and the honey-brown gaze pulled him into their endless sweet depths. Hearing her speak his name, he felt electrified.

"Security!" his butler cried, motioning to a bodyguard on the other side of the room. Alessandro grabbed Bronson's arm.

"I will handle this," he growled. "Thank you."

Mollified, the butler nodded and backed away. "Of course, sir."

Taking Lilley gently by the arm, Alessandro pulled her inside the foyer. She looked up at him, her lips parted.

His hand involuntarily tightened, his fingers trembling at the point of contact against her soft skin. Waves of sensual memories washed over his unwilling body. The last time they'd been together, they'd made love in every room here, including this foyer. He looked at the wall behind her. There.

Suddenly choking with need, he felt an overwhelming drive to carry her up to his bed—to claim her body as his own. He'd thought being away from Lilley would make him forget. It had only made him want her more.

Blood roared in his ears as he reached around her and closed the heavy oak door. Dropping Lilley's arm, he folded his hands to keep himself from touching her. He said hoarsely, "You shouldn't have come."

She took a deep breath. "I had no choice."

"What is she doing here?" Olivia demanded peevishly in English behind him. "Did you invite her, Alessandro?"

Oh yes, Olivia. He'd forgotten her completely. He glanced back at her, irritated. "No, I did not invite her." He turned back to Lilley. "Why are you here?"

Lilley moved closer to him, a soft smile on her lips. Her brown eyes were luminous, catching at his soul. She seemed like a creature from another world, a kinder one filled with magic and innocence. Her pretty face was suffused with a strange glow. "I came to see you."

He stared at her, bewildered. *I came to see you.* No pretense? No games? No story about *just being in the neighborhood?* He hardly knew how to deal with such straightforward, vulnerable honesty. He'd had so little experience with it.

"You weren't invited," Olivia said coldly. "You need to leave."

It was clear by her scowl that she'd recognized Lilley as the woman Alessandro had taken to the Preziosi di Caetani ball. Olivia glared at her as if she hoped the hot laser beam of her eyes might cause the younger woman to burst into flame.

But looking back at Olivia, Lilley's gaze didn't have a shred of anger or even fear. Instead, she looked at the Italian heiress with something almost like…sympathy.

"I'm not here to cause a scene," Lilley said quietly. "I just need to speak to Alessandro, alone. Please. It will only take a moment."

"Alessandro doesn't want to talk to you." When he remained silent, Olivia tossed her head, giving Lilley a nasty glare. "Get out before I throw you out, you cheap little—file clerk."

But her attempted insult seemed to roll right off Lilley like water off a duck's back. She turned back to Alessandro with a soft smile. "May I please speak to you? Alone?"

Being alone with Lilley, mere minutes before he planned to propose to Olivia, was a bad idea. A *very* bad idea. He opened his mouth to tell Lilley firmly that she must go. Instead, his body twisted and he heard himself saying in Italian, "Will you please excuse us?"

Olivia drew back with a hiss between her teeth, visibly furious. "Certainly," she said coldly. "I'll go greet the mayor and my good friend Bill Hocking," she said, referring to a well-known Silicon Valley billionaire. Her warning couldn't have been clearer. But suddenly he didn't give a damn.

"Grazie," he answered mildly, as if utterly oblivious of her affronted fury.

With a scowl, Olivia turned on her heel and stomped away, her bare back looking almost skeletal in the black one-shouldered gown.

Alessandro looked back down at Lilley, who, with her soft body and simple cotton clothes seemed even more impossibly alluring than he remembered.

Amidst all the noise around them, the jazz music, the soft clink of wineglasses and laughter of guests, he felt as if they were alone. "I never expected to see you again," he murmured. "I can't believe you crashed my party."

She smiled. "Really brave of me, right? Or really stupid."

"Brave and stupid are often the same thing."

Lilley shook her head, and he saw unshed tears in her eyes as she laughed. "I'm glad to see you, Alessandro. I've missed you."

Hearing her leave herself so vulnerable, he felt it again—that odd twisting in the vicinity of his heart. "But you shouldn't have come here tonight."

Her eyes met his. "Because this is an engagement party."

Alessandro tried to keep his face blank. "You read gossip magazines."

"Unfortunately."

Bracing himself, he waited for the inevitable scene, for her tears and recriminations. Instead, she just gave him a wistful smile.

"I want you to be happy." She lifted her chin. "If Olivia is truly the one, I wish you all the happiness in the world."

Alessandro's jaw fell open. It was the last thing he'd expected her to say. He took a deep breath, suddenly uncertain how to proceed.

"You—aren't upset?" he said finally. His cheeks became

hot as he heard how foolish the words sounded to his own ears.

"There's no point to being upset over something I cannot change." She stared down at the marble floor. "And I truly didn't come to cause a scene."

"Then why did you?"

She looked up, her eyes luminous and wide. Beneath the darkening light of the upper windows, her eyes were the color of a mountain stream. Not just brown, he realized. Her eyes were a thousand shades, depths of green and blue and amber like a deep, ancient river.

"I have something to tell you before I can leave San Francisco."

Leave? Why on earth would she leave? Then Alessandro remembered he'd convinced a friend to offer her a job in New York. When he'd been in Mexico City, enduring night after night of hot dreams, he'd thought sending her three thousand miles away from San Francisco was the only sane thing to do. Now, he thought it the stupidest idea he'd ever conceived. His shoulders tightened. "Lilley—"

The doorbell rang, and as Bronson hesitantly came towards the door Alessandro grabbed Lilley's hand. He pulled her out of the foyer, away from the hubbub of the party, leading her down a side hall.

"Where are we going?" she asked, not resisting him.

His hand tightened around hers. "Where we can be alone."

Turning down a second hallway towards a quiet wing, Alessandro tried to ignore how right her hand felt in his own, tried not to feel the enticing warmth of her soft skin. But as he pulled her into the music room where he often hosted concerts and parties, the large room suddenly felt small, the temperature hot and stifling. As he walked around the grand piano and past the Picasso on the wall, his tie felt tight around his neck. He just kept walking through the music room. Opening the sliding glass doors, he pulled her into a small private garden.

Outside, the air was cool. The garden was green and stark, just a lawn, really, surrounded on three sides by a ten-foot privet hedge that separated them from the pool-side terrace. On the other side of the hedge, he could hear muffled conversation and the clink of wineglasses as guests milled around the Olympic-size pool and terrace.

Alessandro realized he was still holding Lilley's hand. He looked down at their intertwined fingers. She followed his gaze and he heard her intake of breath, felt her tremble.

Their eyes met in the rapidly deepening twilight. The sky above the villa was dark with threatening clouds, and he heard a distant rumble of thunder. He heard the wind howl through the trees. Lilley's full cotton skirt swirled around her legs.

Electricity filled the air as the temperature seemed to drop five degrees around them. But Alessandro still felt hot, burning from the storm inside him. Desire arced though him, and with an intake of breath, he dropped her hand.

Lilley deserved better than a series of cheap one-night stands. For her sake, he couldn't risk her loving him. And for his own sake…he couldn't risk caring for her. He'd learned long ago to trust no one. Sex and money were real. Love was a lie.

He knew this, but his body shook with the effort of not touching her, from not putting his arms around her and sinking into her softness and warmth. He tightened his hands into fists.

"Why did you come?" he ground out.

Colorful fairy lights high in the trees swayed violently in the rising wind. A flash of lightning illuminated Lilley's stricken face.

"You're in love with Miss Bianchi, aren't you?"

He set his jaw. "I told you. Marriage is a mutually beneficial alliance. Love has nothing to do with it."

"But surely you wouldn't want to spend the rest of your life without love." Long tendrils of soft brown hair blew across her face as she searched his gaze. Her expression faltered. "Would you?"

Thunder crackled in the sky above. Alessandro heard gasps from the other side of the hedge as the first raindrops fell, and guests ran back inside the villa.

"Just tell me what you have to say, then leave," he said tightly.

Lilley blinked, then looked down at the grass beneath her feet. "This is hard. Harder than I ever thought it would be."

Rain began to fall more heavily. He watched a fat raindrop slide down her rounded cheek to her full, generous mouth. Her pink tongue unconsciously darted out to lick the thick drop of rain against her full, sweetly sensual lips, and he nearly groaned.

He had to get her out of here before he did something they'd both regret forever. Why had he ever allowed himself to take a single forbidden taste of what did not belong to him by right?

"It was a mistake for me to seduce you," he said in a low voice. "I'm sorry I ever touched you."

She looked up, her eyes bright with grief. "Was it so awful?"

Awful? A new ache filled his throat. He hated that for the first time in nineteen years, he'd found a heart he did not want to break, and here he was breaking it. "Your first time should have been special, with a man who loved you, who might someday marry you. Not a one-night stand with a man like me."

"Don't be so hard on yourself." She tried to give him a smile. "It was two nights."

He nearly shuddered with the memory of how good it had been between them. How she'd tasted. How she'd felt beneath him. He forced himself to say, "You will find someone else."

She stared at him. "That's why you're sending me to New York."

Thunder boomed over them. "You knew it was me?"

"Of course I knew." She looked at him with a tremulous smile. She swallowed, then squared her shoulders. Rain was starting to soak her long brown hair, causing her tank top and cotton skirt to cling to her skin. "Thank you for arranging the internship. It was—very kind."

Her generous spirit only made Alessandro feel more like a brute. His head was throbbing with pain. He tightened his hands into fists. "I wasn't being kind, damn you. I was sending you away because I'm getting married. Not for love. Her father's company will be an asset." His hands tightened. "But when I speak vows, I will be faithful to them."

Lilley searched his gaze. "And if I were an heiress like her?" she whispered. "Would you choose me as your bride instead?"

Looking at her, he held his breath. Then slowly, he shook his head. "You would never fit into my world." His hand lifted. "It would destroy everything about you that I admire most. Everything that is cheerful and bright."

He barely caught himself before he touched her cheek. Thunder cracked again above their heads, as loud and metallic as a baseball bat against the earth, and he dropped his hand. "Olivia will be my perfect bride."

"I can't let you marry her. Not without knowing what I, what I..." She licked her lips. "What I have to tell you."

Alessandro's suit was now completely wet. The two of them were alone in the emerald garden, below the black sky. The scent of rain washed over the leaves, over the earth, over the distant vineyards and the pink bougainvillea twisting up the stucco of his villa.

And looking at her beautiful, stricken brown eyes, he suddenly knew what she was going to say.

"Don't," he ground out. "Don't say it."

She hesitated, her lovely round face looking scared. Her hair and clothes were now stuck to her skin. He could see the full outline of her breasts and hard jut of her nipples beneath her thin cotton tank top. He could see the shape of her curvaceous legs beneath her skirt as lightning flashed above them. "Alessandro—"

"No, *cara.*" He put his hand to her lips, stroking the rain off her face with the pads of his thumbs. "Please," he whispered. "Do not speak the words. Leave us that, at least. I can see your feelings on your face. I already know what is in your heart."

Lilley looked up at him, her expression breathless. The rain began to fall more heavily and he realized he'd cupped her face in his hands. Her wet, full, pink lips were inches from his own, and he suddenly couldn't breathe. He was hard and aching, his lips pulsing with the drive to kiss her. His body clamored for him to push her roughly against the hedge and claim her as his own.

Using every drop of willpower he possessed, Alessandro dropped his hands, stepping away. He said harshly, "Go to New York, Lilley."

"Wait," she choked out as he turned away. "You can't go. Not until I tell you—"

He whirled to face her, his expression cold. "Do not fight

me. We must never see each other again. There is nothing you can say to make me change my decision."

She took a deep breath.

"I'm pregnant with your baby," she whispered.

CHAPTER SIX

THUNDER pounded the dark sky, shaking the earth beneath her feet. Lilley held her breath, waiting for his reaction.

The violently swinging fairy lights above the hedge caused shadows to move across the sharp planes of Alessandro's handsome face as he said hoarsely, "Pregnant."

"Yes."

A sharp flash of lightning illuminated his grim black eyes as he took a single step towards her. "You can't be."

"I am."

"We used protection."

She spread her arms helplessly. "That one time, in the shower..."

He sucked in his breath. "No."

"But—"

"No." Clawing back his wet black hair, he paced three steps across the lawn. Lilley watched him with a building sense of despair. Her body felt ice-cold, soaked to the bone. But that was nothing compared to her heart. She'd known he didn't want her, and that he wouldn't want their baby. But knowing it in her head and hearing him say it out loud were two different things.

She wrapped her arms around her shivering body, trying to comfort herself and the baby inside her. *It's all right,* she told herself, using the words her mother had often said to her when she was young and sad. *It'll be all right, sweetheart.*

It worked. She felt the anguish give way a fraction inside her. Lifting her head, she looked at Alessandro. She whispered, "It's all right."

He stopped pacing. "What?"

Love was a gift, Lilley realized. Love was always a gift. Even if the person you loved chose not to love you back.

She looked at Alessandro, so handsome and impossibly sexy even with his expensive suit soaked with rain. His dark hair was plastered to his forehead and tousled. Compassion for him, for this man she'd almost loved, filled her heart, crowding out her grief for the husband and father he could never be. She took a deep breath. "Nothing has to change for you."

The expression on his face was suddenly as dark and ominous as the storm. "What?"

"You told me from the start that our affair would only be a fling." She shook her head. "I don't expect you to help me raise our baby. I just thought you should know."

Alessandro's eyes were black. The muscles of his powerful body tightened. "If you don't expect me to raise your child, exactly what do you want from me?"

She blinked. "Want?"

"What are your demands? A house? Money?"

His words were hard, but she saw the tremble of his body beneath the sheeting rain. And Lilley suddenly wondered what sort of people he'd lived with, that his first thought upon hearing she was pregnant was to expect her to demand money.

"I don't need anything," she said quietly. *Except a father for my baby,* came the painful thought. *Except for a man who can love me.* But she would have to be brave, to be both mother and father to her sweet baby, who would need everything she could give. "Thank you for giving me two nights I'll never forget. Thank you for believing in me. And most of all," she whispered over the ache in her throat, "thank you for giving me a baby."

Blinking fast, she looked up at his face for the last time, trying to memorize his features into her memory. The aquiline silhouette of his nose. The hard angle of his jaw. His eyes like dark embers, blazing fire. "I hope your life is full of joy. I'll never forget you." She turned away. "Good-bye."

Lilley started walking back towards the villa, her sandals squishing in the wet grass, her heart breaking.

His hand grabbed her shoulder, whirling her around. He looked down at her as the rain continued to pound them both. His eyes burned with fury. "You think you can tell me you're pregnant—and just *leave?*"

Lilley sucked in her breath, almost frightened at the darkness in his eyes. "There is no reason for me to stay—"

"No reason?" His voice was nearly a shout. He visibly controlled himself. His jaw twitched as he loosened his grip on her upper arms. "If you truly are pregnant with my child," he ground out, "how can you just turn and leave? How can you be so cold?"

"Cold?" she gasped, ripping away. "What do you want from me? You want me to fall to the ground and cling to your knees, begging for you to love me and this baby, begging for you never to let me go?"

"That at least I would understand!"

"I can't change your nature!" she cried, then took a deep gulping breath. "You made your feelings clear. You want a wife you can be proud of. You want Olivia. And you want me three thousand miles away!"

His eyes narrowed as he said in a low voice, "That was before."

"Nothing has changed."

"Everything has changed, if the baby is really mine."

It took several seconds for the meaning of his words to sink in. Then her eyes went wide. "You think I would sleep with another man, then lie to you about it?"

Alessandro's posture was so taut, he seemed like a statue. Like a stone. She could barely hear his voice as he said, "It happens." His expression looked strange. "You might have gone back to the jewelry designer. Accidentally gotten pregnant, than decided to cash in."

"Cash in?" she said incredulously. "Cash in how?"

He searched her gaze. "Do you swear you're telling me the truth? The child is mine?"

"Of course the baby is yours! You're the only man I've ever slept with in my whole life!"

"I want a paternity test."

She stiffened. "What?"

"You heard me."

The insult was almost too much to bear. "Forget it," she whispered. "I'm not doing some stupid paternity test. If you trust me so little, if you believe I'd lie to you about something like this, then just forget it."

Lilley's body shook as she turned and walked away. Tears streamed down her face, blending with the rain. She was halfway across the empty lawn before he stopped her, and this time, the expression on his face had changed.

"I'm sorry, Lilley," he said quietly. "I do know you. And you wouldn't lie."

Their eyes locked. She exhaled as the knots in her shoulders loosened. Then he spoke.

"Marry me."

She heard the roar of her own heartbeat above the splatter of rain. "Is that a joke?"

His sensual lips curved upward. "I never joke, remember?"

Her head was spinning. She'd never expected him to propose, not in a million years, not in her most delusional dreams. "You…want to marry me?"

"Is that so surprising? What did you expect—that I'd kick you and our unborn child to the curb and merrily go and propose to another woman?"

Biting her lip, she looked up at the ruthless lines of his face. "Well…yes."

"Then you don't know me at all."

"No," she whispered. "I guess I don't." She felt dizzy and still a bit sick. She'd barely made it to Sonoma in Nadia's old car without being sick, she'd been so nervous. And now he wanted to marry her? She licked her lips, feeling as though she might cry. "You want to help raise our baby?"

Alessandro's jaw was tight. "I will protect you both. I will give the baby my name. It is my duty."

Her heart, which had been soaring in blind hope, crashed to the ground. His *duty?* She exhaled. "You don't need to marry me to be involved in our baby's life."

"Yes. I do."

"Why?"

"Because it is necessary."

"You're old-fashioned."

"Yes."

"But you don't love me!"

He folded his arms. "Irrelevant."

"Not to me, it isn't!" She exhaled, clenching her hands. "Listen, Alessandro, I'll never try to keep you from seeing your child—"

"I know that you will not, once we are wed."

"I'm not going to marry you!"

"Of course you will," he said coldly.

She shook her head, causing wet tendrils to slap against

her cheeks. "Be in a loveless marriage for the rest of my life? No thanks!"

"I understand. You still want your knight in shining armor." He set his jaw. "But whatever either of us might have once planned for our lives is over. We are expecting a child. We will wed."

"No—we would be miserable!"

"Miserable?" he said incredulously. "Don't you understand? You will be my bride. A princess. Rich beyond your wildest dreams!"

"I don't care—I don't want it! Not when I know you don't love me and never will!"

He grabbed her by the shoulders, his hands sliding against her wet skin. "You would deny our child a name out of some childish yearning for fairytale dreams?"

"It's not childish." She closed her eyes, which suddenly burned with tears that he'd used his knowledge of her heart against her. "You are cruel."

"I am *right,*" he said grimly. "You have no reason to refuse me." He paused. "I will even be faithful to you, Lilley."

He spoke the words as if being faithful to her would require a huge sacrifice, practically more than any billionaire prince could bear. And it was probably true. "Gee, thanks," she said sarcastically, glaring at him. "But I have no interest in being your duty bride."

"Your objection is to the word *duty?*" He narrowed his eyes. "What do you think marriage is?"

"Love. Friendship. Having each other's backs. A poetic union of souls—"

His grip on her tightened. "And passion?" His voice became husky beneath the rain. "What of passion?"

Her heart fell to her sandals and back again. She felt his strength, his warmth, the irresistible pull of his power. Against her will, she craved him.

"It was good between us." He ran his fingers lightly along her jawline, his thumb along her sensitive lower lip. His soft stroke caused a spark down her body that made her suck in her breath. "You know how it was."

Memories shuddered through her of how it had felt when he'd made love to her. Her breasts felt heavy, her nipples aching and tight. She swallowed. "It was a fling," she breathed. "You said so yourself. I'm not the right woman to be your bride."

"My assessment has changed." He cupped her face. His eyes were dark with heat. "For the last month," he whispered, "I've thought of nothing but having you in my bed."

She licked her lips. "You—you have?"

"I told myself you deserved a man who could love you. But everything has changed. Only our child matters now." His gaze fell to her lips. "But that's a lie," he said in a low voice. "That's not the only reason I want you as my bride. I want you to be mine. I want to possess you completely. Every night. For the rest of our lives."

Lilley could barely breathe. "But Olivia—"

"I would have married her out of duty. Not desire." He looked into her eyes. "You are the one I want, Lilley." His mouth lowered to hers with agonizing slowness as he whispered, "Don't you know that by now? I want you. And now I will have you—forever."

As he kissed her, she closed her eyes, her body shaking as his lips took ruthless possession of her own. His lips were hard and hungry as the rain poured over their skin and thunder pounded across the lowering black sky.

She heard his low growl as in a sudden movement he pushed her back against the hedge. She felt the rough, wet branches of the shrubbery against her back as he held her tight against his wet, muscled body. He moved his hands through her hair, tilting her head to deepen the kiss. In the force of their embrace, their wet clothes slid and clung to their skin. His hands roamed everywhere, over her cotton tank top, over her hips. She felt his hand reach beneath the hemline of her skirt, dragging it slowly up her thighs. His hand slid upwards, and she gasped, placing her hand over his. "No."

"Don't refuse me," he said in a low voice. "It's what we both want."

"I do want you," she panted, then choked out a sob. "But I can't marry you. I'd have to give up everything I believe in. I'm afraid it would destroy me to love you."

"So don't love me." He caressed her hair, looking down at her with serious dark eyes. "It's too late for our own dreams, Lilley," he said quietly. "All that matters now are our baby's."

She sucked in her breath. He was right, she realized. All that mattered now was their child. She closed her eyes. "Will you love our baby? Will you be a good father?"

"Yes," he said simply.

Her heart twisted as she took a deep breath, then another. For an instant, she held her breath. Then she let her dreams for love go.

She opened her eyes.

"I can accept…a marriage without love," she whispered, then shook her head. "But not without trust. Not without respect. I won't be humiliated by a paternity test. Either believe that the baby is yours…or let us go."

Staring at her, Alessandro slowly nodded. "All right, *cara,*" he said in a low voice. "All right."

Swallowing back the ache in her throat, she whispered, "Then I'll marry you."

Alessandro drew back. "You will?" The rain had lifted, and a beam of twilight sun burst from behind the clouds, illuminating his hard features with gold. "You'll be my wife?"

Wordlessly, she nodded.

His eyes lit up, and the edges of his lips curved up into a bright smile that made him look younger, almost boyish. She'd never seen him look that way before. As Lilley stared up at him, the noise of the storm faded, and thunder became a distant memory.

Maybe it would be all right, she thought, dazed. Maybe passion and a baby would be enough to start a marriage.

She prayed it would be. Because that was all they had.

CHAPTER SEVEN

LILLEY's hair flew around her, tangling in the cold night wind as Alessandro drove his yellow Ferrari convertible across the vast, lonely Nevada desert. She couldn't stop looking over at him at the wheel. Moonlight frosted his dark hair with silver.

The party had ended in scandal, when Alessandro had privately informed Olivia that she'd been misled by the gossip columns and he intended to take Lilley as his bride. Olivia had stomped out of the villa, but not before she'd grabbed Lilley's arm in the foyer.

"You'll regret this," the beautiful Milanese heiress had hissed, pressing her fingernails into Lilley's flesh. "You might be pregnant with his child, you piece of trash, but you're not worthy to be his wife. You think you've beaten me. But I will find a way to destroy you."

Turning, the gorgeous blonde had departed, her skinny shoulders straight as she'd stormed out of the villa. In the next room Alessandro was already announcing their engagement to all of his friends, introducing them to Lilley at his side. They'd applauded and murmured congratulations, but she'd felt their bewildered eyes on her, as if they were wondering why on earth someone like Alessandro would choose her for his bride. Something she kept wondering herself. Then he'd announced with a wicked smile, "We're eloping to Las Vegas. Tonight."

Lilley had gasped along with everyone else. They would drive to Las Vegas, he insisted, as his private jet was en route to San Francisco after delivering supplies to a desperate community decimated by a hurricane. "We'll be married by morning," Alessandro had told her after he'd gotten rid of the guests. He paused. "Unless you wish to wait until your father can attend the ceremony…"

She'd felt a prickle at the back of her neck, knowing she had to tell Alessandro the truth about her family before they could possibly marry. She shook her head. "No. I don't want my father at the ceremony, and you wouldn't either. We're not exactly friends. I'm not even sure he loves me." She took a deep breath. "Speaking of which," she said in a small voice, "there's something I need to tell you. Before I can marry you."

"No need." His expression had suddenly become cold, closed off. "I already know what you're going to say."

Alessandro knew about her family? Her jaw dropped. "You—you do?"

He nodded, his eyes hard. "There's no point in talking about it, because there's nothing I can do to change it."

She bit her lip. "So you—you forgive me?" she whispered.

"Yes," he said grimly, then shook his head. "But I will never be able to love you."

Lilley wasn't worried about him loving her at that moment. She'd just been praying he wouldn't utterly despise her. Relief washed through her. He knew her secret. Of course he did, she thought, suddenly so giddy she was almost light-headed. He'd probably known it all along! Alessandro Caetani was a brilliant competitor, which is why her cousin found him to be such an infuriating foe. He knew stuff. With a tearful, joyful sob, she threw her arms around him.

Surprised, he'd put his arms around her. "I'll have my people pack up your things and meet us in Las Vegas. No need to pack clothes," he'd said gruffly. "I'll provide you with those."

"I need my jewelry materials and tools, and the quilt my mother made me."

"You have a passport, yes?"

"Yes." With a whole bunch of stamps in and out of French airports she wouldn't have to hide. "Why a passport?"

"I have a little place in Sardinia." He'd smiled, his eyes hot. "A honeymoon cottage."

They drove all night in his convertible, across the dark, vast Nevada desert. Sometime during the night, she'd fallen asleep against his shoulder. When they arrived in Las Vegas, Alessandro woke her with a kiss to her forehead.

"Welcome to your wedding day, *cara,*" he whispered, and she opened her eyes blearily to see the white light of dawn breaking over the distant craggy mountains.

Alessandro took her to the luxury Hermitage Hotel and Resort, where he ordered a lavish private buffet for two brought up to their penthouse suite. Five waiters with overflowing carts brought up fifty different items for Lilley to sample—waffles, omelets, pecan-stuffed French toast, slabs of bacon, watermelon, fruit salad and chicken-fried steak. Afterward, Alessandro escorted her to an overpriced bridal boutique downstairs in the hotel. Selecting a tuxedo for himself, he casually bought the first wedding dress she admired.

"You can't!" Lilley cried when she saw the twenty-thousand-dollar price tag, even as her eyes traced the beaded white fabric longingly.

Lifting his eyebrow, he gave her a grin. "I can."

They collected their marriage license downtown, then returned to their suite at the Hermitage where a bridal bouquet and boutonniere waited for them beside the grand piano. It was intoxicating. Dreamy. They made love on the huge bed overlooking the Las Vegas Strip, then made love again in the shower before changing their clothes. Then, when Alessandro first saw Lilley in her wedding dress, he pulled her straight back into bed.

Lilley sat astride his lap, riding him as he leaned against the headboard, her necklace bouncing softly against her swollen breasts with every thrust. After their third lust-fueled explosion of the afternoon, he kissed the necklace's pink-heart crystal and brass chain. "Any man on earth would pay a fortune to have such a necklace for his wife." His expression changed. "It's just too bad that…"

"What?"

He exhaled. "Nothing." Taking her hand, he pulled her from the bed. "Let's get to the ceremony before we get distracted."

Two hours after their appointed time, they finally married, surrounded by white candles at the hotel's private wedding chapel. An acquaintance of Alessandro's who owned the hotel, Nikos Stavrakis, was the only witness as they breathlessly spoke their vows.

And just like that, Lilley was a princess. Wearing a white suit he'd purchased for her, she boarded her husband's waiting jet, bound for the Mediterranean.

On board, Lilley found the possessions his staff had packed for her. The box of her life was small indeed—just her mother's homemade quilt, her jewelry tools and an excited, gushing note from Nadia wishing her luck and all the joy in the world. "Jeremy will be moving in with me now—I know you won't mind because you're a happily married princess! I can't believe you *married* Prince Alessandro! You'll be famous now!"

As the jet flew the long miles east across the country and towards the Atlantic, Lilley fell asleep on a couch, holding her mother's quilt to her chest. When she woke up, Alessandro was watching her from a nearby white leather chair.

"I will always protect you," he whispered, leaning forward. His eyes were dark. "I want you to know that. And I will protect our child."

She sat up, clutching the quilt. "Protect us. But not too much." She gave him a weak smile. "My father tried to protect me from the world he didn't think I was strong enough to handle. If not for my mother, I would never have been allowed out of the house."

"Which is why he wanted you to marry one of his employees." His lips lifted in a humorless smile. "When will you tell him about our marriage?"

Her eyes slid away. "I don't know. It's—complicated."

"I understand." He looked down at his folded hands. "My father married my mother for her money, then spent it all on his mistresses, whom he flaunted to her face. He thought condoms were for the weak. He scattered bastards carelessly all over the world."

She sucked in her breath. "Oh, Alessandro—"

He looked up, his handsome face stoic. "He died when I was nineteen, and left us only debts in his memory. My mother would have starved in the street, if I hadn't started work to support her. When she died five years ago, she was living in a palace in Rome. As I vowed she someday would." He exhaled. "I'm trying to tell you that you never need to worry now, about anything. I will always take care of you."

She blinked back tears, giving him a smile as she reached

across the aisle to stroke his face. "We will take care of each other."

He turned his rough cheek into her caress, then placed his hand over her own. "You won't regret giving up your dreams to marry me. I'm no shining knight, but I will treat you well. You won't have a business of your own, but I will work hard for you and the baby. I'll give you all the precious jewelry you could possibly desire."

Frowning, she drew back her hand. "What do you mean—giving up my dream of having a business?"

He stared down at her. "You have no time for a career. Not anymore. Your place is to be my wife, and raise our child."

"You don't tell me this until *now*—after we're already married?"

"I thought it would be obvious," he said stiffly, looking uncomfortable.

"No," she whispered. "You knew I would be upset. Which is why you waited till now." She forced her voice to be calm. "I never agreed to give up my business."

He looked at her. "If that dream had ever meant anything to you, you would have done something about it long ago."

Lilley's eyes widened, then she sucked in her breath. He was right. She could have built her business for years, but instead, she'd squandered her time being paralyzed by fear.

"Money will never be an issue for you again," he tried. "I will provide you with everything you desire." He gave her a smile. "And if you want to make jewelry as a little hobby to entertain yourself, I have no objection to it."

"Generous of you," she muttered.

He stared down at her, then set his jaw. "Once you have properly settled in as my bride, as the mother of our child, well then—we will see," he said grudgingly. His eyes softened as he stroked her cheek. "I want you to be happy, Lilley. I will do everything I can to make that happen."

Feeling his hand upon her skin, seeing the tenderness in his eyes, she exhaled. It would be fine. Somehow, it would all work out. "I want to do the same for you."

His eyes were hot and dark as he gave her a wicked grin. "Ah, but you've made me so happy already. You make me happy on an hourly basis," he breathed, leaning forward to kiss her. He stopped, his face inches from hers. "Just promise you'll never lie to me."

"I'll never lie to you," Lilley promised, and she meant it, with all her heart.

"Io bacio."

"Io bacio," Lilley repeated, balancing a book on her head.

Standing by the window overlooking the bright-blue water of the Costa Smeralda, her Italian tutor smiled. *"Tu baci."*

"Tu baci," Lilley repeated rather breathlessly, walking across the marble floor in four-inch high heels.

"Lui bacia."

As Lilley repeated all the conjugations of *baciare,* she found herself smiling. Her tutor had clearly chosen the verb *to kiss* in honor of her standing as a newlywed. And though her feet ached from the expensive shoes and her body ached from standing up straight in the designer skirt suit for hours, she felt strangely happy. Yes, her head ached from a full schedule of etiquette and deportment lessons, mixed with Italian classes in which she not only learned the word for fork, *la forchetta,* but she was taught which one to use for salad and which for dessert. But she was…happy.

This wasn't the same world she'd left behind in Minnesota, that was for sure. Her father had come from nothing. He'd never given a hoot about etiquette. Now, after a week in Sardinia, Lilley felt exhausted, but it was the best kind of tired. She felt sore, too, but there was a very delicious reason for that as well. A hot blush filled her cheeks as she remembered what Alessandro had done to her in bed last night, and what she'd done to him. The braver she got, the more she acted on her own needs and fantasies, the more he liked it.

"Molto bene," the Italian tutor finally said with satisfaction.

"You are a quick learner, *Principessa,*" said the Swiss woman who'd come from a famous boarding school in the Alps to teach her deportment.

"Grazie," Lilley said with a laugh. A quick learner? She'd certainly never heard *that* one before. But it helped that she didn't have to read, just listen, repeat and practice. Her husband had given the instructors precise instructions.

Her husband.

After a week in Alessandro's white wedding-cake villa in Sardinia, seven blissful days of life as his wife, Lilley still adored the word *husband.* She held the word close to her heart, cuddled it like a child. She had a *husband.* And—she glanced discreetly at her watch, almost causing the book to slide off her head—it was almost five o'clock. Her favorite time of day.

The Italian tutor followed her gaze and nodded. "We are done." He turned to gather his briefcase. *"Buona sera, Principessa."*

Madame Renaud pulled the leatherbound book off Lilley's head. *"Bonsoir, Principessa,"* she said, *"et merci."* Madame followed her tutor out of the door.

Principessa. Another word that still seemed exotic and foreign—nothing to do with her at all.

The instant her instructors were gone, Lilley raced upstairs towards the master bedroom as fast as her tight beige pencil skirt would allow her. She rushed down the hall, past priceless works of modern art that to her looked like a preschooler's squiggles, past expensive white furniture that was mostly just hard and uncomfortable in her opinion.

But there was one thing about this villa that she loved: their bedroom. Her high heels clicked loudly as she hurried down the hall. Passing a window, her eyes fell on the view of the turquoise Mediterranean and white sand beach. All right—two things she loved about this house.

A week ago she would have had difficulty placing the Italian island of Sardinia on a map, but now she was in love, because the Costa Smeralda, the island's green coast, was the most joyful and beautiful place she'd ever seen. The open windows lured in a warm, sweet wind to blow against her hair, and the bright golden sun warmed her body and heart. As if those needed any warming.

Running her hand along the curving handrail of the villa's white staircase, she snorted as she remembered Alessandro's description of this vacation home. Some *cottage!* It had eight bedrooms and a full staff, though they always disappeared at five o'clock each night, as Alessandro had ordered, so the two of them could be alone.

Lilley smiled to herself. She enjoyed her lessons during the day, but at night…She shivered. At night, she and her husband set the world on fire.

At the end of the hallway, Lilley pushed open their bedroom door, half expecting to find Alessandro on the bed, wearing only a strategically placed jewelry box. Yesterday, he'd worn only a large black velvet box which held a priceless diamond and emerald necklace. He seemed to enjoy giving her such expensive trinkets, so Lilley always tried to accept them graciously, even though the impersonal, sterile new jewelry was the last thing she cared about.

Spending time in bed with him, on the other hand…well. She'd take all of that she could get.

But today, their bedroom was empty. So was the study where Alessandro had had business meetings all day with high-level board members from his headquarters in Rome. Peeking through the window, she saw him pacing by the pool, talking on the phone. Lilley's eyes devoured his strong physique in a snug white T-shirt, old jeans and bare feet as he paced from the white cabana to the poolhouse. Behind him, palm trees waved against the sparkling blue sea.

The pool! Perfect! She'd get him splashing in there yet!

Squelching a mischievous laugh, Lilley raced back to their bedroom and changed into a tiny bikini, one of the six he'd bought for her in Porto Cervo. Tying the strings at her hips and back, she glanced at herself in the mirror. Funny how she'd once felt so embarrassed about her plump body. She'd worn baggy clothes that didn't fit, trying to hide her shape. But Alessandro loved her body so much, what could possibly be wrong with it? How could she not love her overlarge breasts, her curvy belly, her wide hips, with their child growing inside her?

For the first time in her life, she felt comfortable in her own skin. Even the morning sickness had all but disappeared since she'd become Alessandro's wife. A coincidence? Or were her body and unborn baby in agreement with her, all of them deliriously happy about their new lives?

Lilley looked at the brilliant ten-carat canary diamond ring on her finger. He'd bought it for her at the Caetani boutique in Las Vegas, as if the million-dollar price tag were nothing at all. It was pretty, though it weighed down her hand. As she went outside, the facets sparkled. She saw her husband sitting in a chair by the pool with a computer in his lap, and he was more seductive to her than any diamond.

His dark form shone brighter than the white sun, which on Sardinia was really saying something.

Palm trees waved in the warm breeze, giving a hint of moving shade over Alessandro as she walked around the pool, swaying her hips.

He didn't look up, but continued to stare intently at the screen. She went around to the back of his chair, then bent to rub his shoulders. "Hi."

"Buon pomeriggio, cara," he said absently, typing.

"Buon pomeriggio?" Smiling, she shook her head. *"Buona sera."*

His expression still distracted, Alessandro glanced up at her. Then he got a good look at her bikini, and his eyes widened. He snapped his computer shut. *"Buona sera,"* he replied with interest. "Your Italian is coming along."

"I've always been interested in your native tongue," she said with a suggestive smile. When she saw his gaze linger upon her breasts, she glanced innocently at his computer. "I'm sorry to interrupt, were you done?"

"I am now," he growled. Pushing the computer to a side table, he pulled her into his lap and thoroughly kissed her. As she felt his sun-warmed lips against hers, melting her from the inside, she closed her eyes and breathed in his scent. With his body against hers in the sunlight, she felt intoxicated with pleasure.

There was only one thing that bothered her.

For the last week, they'd made love constantly, eaten delicious meals, slept in each other's arms. Last night, he'd taken her into the village for dinner, and afterward he'd held her hand as they walked through the winding streets. She'd thought she might die of happiness. Then they'd strolled past an outdoor nightclub. She'd eagerly tried to pull him towards the music, towards the dancing couples spilling out onto the street. But he'd shaken his head. "I don't dance. You know that."

"Oh, please," she'd cajoled. "Just this once!"

But he'd refused. Except when they were in bed, Alessandro didn't allow himself to do anything that might make him appear vulnerable or foolish. He didn't dance. He didn't *play*. He didn't splash in the pool.

But that was about to change. It was time he learned to let himself go.

Playfully, Lilley pulled away from his embrace. "I need some cooling off."

She walked over to the pool's steps, swaying her hips as she waded slowly into the pool, relishing the shock of cool water against her skin. She went deeper, until the water level bobbed at her breasts. Then she glanced at Alessandro out of the corner of her eye. Oh yeah. He was watching, all right. With a soft, innocent sigh, she sank all the way into the water, swimming with long, sensual strokes. She bobbed up to the edge of the pool, at the foot of Alessandro's chair.

"Join me," she suggested, smiling up at him.

Looking down at her, Alessandro slowly shook his head. "Not my thing."

Languorously, she dipped her hair back in the pool. She felt his burning gaze as she lifted her head from the water. Droplets trickled down her skin, down her neck and breasts. She stretched her arms over her head, moving her body in a lazy sway against the translucent water.

"Join me," she sighed.

He looked as if he were having trouble breathing. Licking his lips, he shook his head.

Lilley sank fully beneath the water and was down there for several seconds. When she finally resurfaced, he'd half risen from his chair as if alarmed. She swam to the edge of the pool, a sensual smile curving her lips. Leaning against the edge, she threw something at his feet. He looked down at it.

It was her bikini.

"Join me," she whispered.

Alessandro looked at her, his lips slightly parted. She heard the hoarse intake of his breath.

Then he moved. She'd never known any man could move that fast. Still dressed in his T-shirt and jeans, he did a cannonball right into the pool beside her. The water swayed wildly, splashing Lilley's head and face as he rose to the surface, throwing back his dark head like a god of the sea. His wet, translucent white T-shirt clung to his shoulders, pecs and tight abs.

Swimming over to her, he grabbed the edge of the pool with one hand, and with the other, he pulled her against him without a word. Lowering his head, he kissed her in a hot, hungry embrace. As his lips seared hers, his tongue teased inside her mouth, and she blindly reached out to the side of the pool to steady herself. Treading water with his powerful legs, he cupped her face with both his hands, deepening the kiss. A sigh of pleasure escaped her. Lost in the moment, Lilley flung both her arms around his shoulders, letting go of the edge.

She had an instant of weightlessness, of swirling pleasure with no beginning or end, as they sank together into the water. Falling, falling, they held tight together in the intensity of their embrace before his legs suddenly kicked beneath them, bringing them back to the surface.

Gripping the edge of the pool, they coughed water out of their lungs. When they could breathe again, they stared at each other, both of them bobbing in the cool water. The white sun beat down on them, reflecting glittering light against the sky and their tanned skin.

Leaning forward, Alessandro pushed her against the

edge of the pool, splaying his large hands over hers. He kissed her deeply, plundering her mouth. Tilting back her head, Lilley closed her eyes, feeling the heat of his mouth and the sun on her skin. Cool ripples of water moved against her naked breasts as he kissed her throat, nipping her shoulder, suckling the tender flesh of her ear.

"Mi piace stare con te," he whispered. *I like being with you.*

"Baciami," she whispered. *Kiss me.*

With a muttered groan, Alessandro turned around in the water. Pulling her arms around his shoulders, he lifted her onto his back and swam towards the steps of the pool. Her naked breasts pressed against his shoulder blades, her body rubbing against his clingy white T-shirt. As he climbed up the steps of the pool, water poured from his shirt and jeans that clung to his powerful body. He pulled her into his arms and looked down at her. There was a strange expression in his dark, handsome face. One she'd never seen before.

"Mia moglie," he whispered. "My sweet wife."

He carried her across the terrace and into the white villa, trailing water with every step. From a distance, she heard seagulls crying and the honking horns of boats. She breathed in the scent of lemon and orange groves mixed with chlorine from the pool and the salt of the sea. She placed her hand on his wet cotton shirt. It revealed every hard muscle of his torso, and she could feel the beat of his heart.

Inside the villa, it was cool, dark and quiet. The housekeeper and other staff had already left for the evening, going back to their homes in nearby villages. She and Alessandro were alone as he carried her up the stairs to their bedroom, to the enormous bed with the sleek white duvet.

The verandah doors were wide open. The wind blew in from the sea, causing the curtains to oscillate slowly in the breeze as Alessandro set her down on their marriage bed, where she'd already had endless revelations of pleasure and joy.

Never looking away from her face, he slowly pulled off his T-shirt, revealing his muscular, tanned chest and broad arms. His jeans and silk boxers were next, as he stripped the wet fabric off his body and left them on the cool marble floor in a crumpled heap. Naked, he moved beside her on the bed.

His kiss was hot and hard, like the rest of him. Then his embrace grew tender, his lips gentling as he whispered words of adoration in Italian that she only half understood, but that caused her to tremble. He pulled away, looking down at her in the shadowy bedroom, and she could hear their breath mingling in the silence. An inexplicable ache of emotion rose to the back of Lilley's throat.

Reaching up, she put her hand on his rough, scratchy cheek.

I love you.

But she couldn't speak the words. She couldn't be that reckless, or that brave.

Alessandro made love to her slowly, taking his time as he caressed and licked and worshipped every inch of her body, until she exploded in the same instant that he groaned and filled her with his seed. Afterward, they held each other. For several minutes, he slept, and she watched him, looking at the contented smile tracing his sensual mouth. She turned towards the open verandah and the translucent curtains swaying peacefully in the breeze. She could see the distant glint of sunlight sparkling like diamonds against the blue water. And she could no longer deny it, not even to herself.

She'd fallen in love with Alessandro. Fallen? The truth was she'd been in love with Alessandro Caetani from the night he'd found her alone and crying in his office that Saturday night.

Lilley's fingertips stroked the dark hair of his chest. He'd brought her pleasure that she never even knew existed. But was she doomed to love a man who would forever give her expensive jewels instead of his heart? Was there anything she could do to win Alessandro's love?

She thought of the etiquette lessons, the Italian lessons, the designer clothes he'd chosen for her. He was changing her completely, and if she were honest with herself, she didn't like all the changes. Her jewelry tools were collecting dust, and except for her wedding gown, he hadn't allowed her to choose a single item of clothing on her own. Other than the jewelry she had made, nothing she wore was truly hers. He dressed her like a doll. He didn't trust her taste, or her ability to fit into his world.

Lilley took a deep breath. She could live with that, she told herself. She'd be the wife he wanted. She'd keep her mouth shut and focus on being elegant and restrained. She'd try harder at her lessons and wear the clothes he wanted her to wear. She would be whomever he wanted her to be, if it would win his love.

Then it would all be worth it—wouldn't it?

Suddenly shivering, she nestled closer into Alessandro's warmth. In a moment, his eyes would open, and he'd lazily suggest dinner, or perhaps he'd want to make love to her again.

Whatever it took. She would convince him to give her the tiniest fraction of his heart, as she'd recklessly given him all of hers. And it would be enough. She would make it be enough. With a deep breath, Lilley squeezed her eyes shut.

Somehow, she would make him love her.

CHAPTER EIGHT

"STOP him. I don't care how, just stop him!"

Sitting at his desk, Alessandro nearly shouted with fury before he hung up on his company's chief financial officer. Clawing back his hair with a silent snarl, he lifted his hand to throw his phone across his study. Then he stopped himself, clutching the cold metal tightly in his hand.

Exhaling, he set the phone carefully on his desk. Rising to his feet, he paced in front of the window, swearing at Théo St. Raphaël in English and Italian and tossing in a few profanities in French, too, for good measure. Damned vulture. Their rivalry had begun years ago when the Frenchman had bought the Italian firm next door to Caetani Worldwide's headquarters in Rome. The insult had deepened when St. Raphaël had stolen the Joyería deal a month ago. But this was the final straw. The man was brazenly making a play for the takeover of a Japanese company that Alessandro needed to deepen his reach in Asia.

Alessandro growled. He'd spent years building up contacts in Tokyo, in hopes of someday gaining control of the firm. And St. Raphaël had no reason to buy the company. It was pure retaliation for Alessandro's purchase of the French vineyard. It was a taunt, pure and simple.

He must be imagining he smelled Alessandro's blood in the water after the humiliation in Mexico City.

And why wouldn't he? *Someone had betrayed him.* Alessandro's chief financial officer had discovered why Miguel Rodriguez had sold Joyería to St. Raphaël instead of Caetani Worldwide. The Frenchman had learned of his plan to close the Mexico City studio and move it to San Francisco. Rodriguez had sold Joyería to the Frenchman to protect his employees' jobs.

But how had St. Raphaël possibly known?

Sitting heavily at his desk, Alessandro stared at his computer. He'd been working with his team remotely as best he could, but the Tokyo deal was spinning out of control, and that was causing problems. He needed to end his honeymoon early and return to Rome.

Alessandro glanced out of the window, instinctively looking for Lilley. It was past five o'clock. She'd come into his study an hour ago, but he'd sent her away—something he'd had to do too often in the last two days. He'd spent a few hours in bed with her last night, then he'd returned to his study to discuss strategy with his Hong Kong office. Last night he'd fallen asleep over his keyboard.

Alessandro exhaled. He should have gone back to Rome two days ago. By remaining in Sardinia, away from his team, he'd put a woman ahead of his business. Something he'd never done before.

But this wasn't just any woman, it was his wife.

There. He spied Lilley on the beach far below. A smile curved his lips and his shoulders unconsciously relaxed as he watched her frolic in the surf, dressed in one of the bikinis he'd bought her in Porto Cervo. Today the color was violet. He saw her pause and look up towards the sprawling white villa, as if she felt him watching her. Visibly squaring her shoulders, she went to talk to some children playing a distance down the beach. He squinted. He vaguely recognized a dark-haired young boy and small girl, the children of live-in servants from the next villa down the coastline. Lilley flopped down on the sand beside them and started enthusiastically to help build their sand castle.

He watched her as she played on the beach. She was so happy, so natural, so free, so good with children. He'd seen the sweet, tender look in her eyes whenever she spoke to him of dreams for their unborn child. Lilley was everything a man would want in a wife. Everything he'd want the mother of his children to be.

She had only one flaw. She loved him.

She'd very nearly confessed her love before their wedding, but he'd seen on her face what she was going to say and stopped her. He exhaled. As long as the words were never said, they had a chance. They could be lovers, even friends. Once the child was born, Lilley would channel her love into their baby. She would raise their child with a mother's tenderness, while Alessandro would protect them and provide for them, ensuring his children would inherit a vast empire.

His wife and children would never be poor. Never be ashamed of their father. His behavior would be above reproach.

He regretted the shabby wedding he'd given Lilley, in the chapel of a Las Vegas casino, with no family and friends. It had been shabby indeed, but expedient and quiet. He had to give Lilley time to complete her lessons, to be fully polished like a hard-edged gemstone before he exposed her to the cutting, subtle mockery of his friends, or the people who passed for his friends. It was the only way to protect her, helping her become strong enough to protect herself.

No man he knew in Rome would have married a pregnant mistress. He would have simply paid her off with a generous check and perhaps a few gifts at the child's birth.

But Alessandro had always vowed his children would

know who their father was. After his own father's selfish, callous example, and even more after his mother's sickening revelation after his death, Alessandro had known the risk of sex, and so he'd waited until he was truly in love. When he'd fallen hard for a twenty-five-year-old waitress in his freshman year at Stanford, he'd taken his time, wooing her for months like a perfect gentleman. Until Heather had dragged him to her apartment and begged him to make love to her. She'd told him he didn't need a condom, because she was on the Pill.

"You trust me, don't you?" she'd asked with big eyes. After so many years of waiting, sex had been a revelation. He'd been rapturous with joy. When she'd gotten pregnant, it had seemed like a miracle.

Until his father died, leaving a shocking amount of debt and creditors all suddenly clamoring to be paid. Alessandro had dropped out of Stanford, planning to get a job to support his mother, and to propose immediately to Heather, so she'd know he intended to take care of her and the baby. He'd rehearsed his speech the night he planned to propose. They'd be poor at first, he would say, but he would work full-time by day and invest every penny he could. Someday, he would promise, he'd give her the life of a princess.

He bought a cheap ring he could ill afford and made her a picnic, preparing bologna sandwiches and fruit salad to eat in the park. But things didn't go according to plan. As he gave her the speech, Heather was silent, setting down her sandwich barely tasted. Afterward, he took her out dancing, his favorite thing to do. He was trying to show her how romantic their lives could be, even without money.

But in the middle of the first song, Heather had stopped on the dance floor. She'd looked up at him, her eyes full of tears.

"I like you, Alessandro," she'd whispered. "I really do.

You're lots of fun and an amazing, generous lover." She exhaled. "But the baby's not yours. I lied."

"Not…" He staggered back. It felt like a physical blow. "Not mine?"

She flushed. "You kept saying you wanted us to wait for true love and all that. But I'm sorry, I couldn't go for two long months without sex!" At his expression, her cheeks colored and she looked away. "The first night we slept together, I already knew I was pregnant."

The loud dance music roared in his ears. His throat closed. "But why?"

"I thought you would make a good husband. A good father." She bit her lip. "The other guy's married. He'll never marry me or help raise the baby. But he owns a tech firm in Cupertino. If I tell him, I know he'll give me money." She'd looked at Alessandro beneath the flashing lights and pulsing music. "I don't want my baby to be poor," she'd whispered. "I'm sorry."

And just like that, she'd left him on the dance floor.

It was the last time Alessandro had ever gone dancing or made a fool of himself over anyone. The last time he'd fully trusted a woman.

Until Lilley.

He could have chosen not to marry her. She'd gone out of her way to make it easy for him to abandon her. She'd apparently had zero expectations of his moral character. It had astonished and angered him. Of course he wished to marry the mother of his unborn baby.

Although he hadn't insisted on that paternity test.

A cold trickle went down his spine. He didn't have any actual proof the baby was his. His hand felt clammy as he forked his fingers through his hair. Lilley wouldn't lie to him, he told himself. He didn't need a paternity test, and he wouldn't insult her by asking for one. Lilley had been a virgin before he'd seduced her, and if she said he was the father, he was. End of story.

"Alessandro? Are you still in here?"

He turned in his swivel chair to see Lilley leaning against the door frame. Her hip was jutted out, her plump breasts overflowing the violet bikini top. His mouth felt dry as he surveyed her full, bare thighs and the hourglass curves of her body. His gaze traced down her long, curvy legs and back up to her swelling, pregnant breasts. He was hard in a millisecond.

"Still working, after all this time?" she murmured, smiling as if she had no idea what the sway of her hips did to him as she walked towards him. "Haven't you heard the adage—all work and no play?"

His little wife had become remarkably adept at the art of seduction in the nine days they'd been married. Still smiling, she put her hand on his shoulder, rubbing his neck. "You said you'd join me on the beach an hour ago."

He looked back at her. "I said no such thing."

"You could be building sandcastles with me."

"Running around, kicking the waves? Not interested."

She shook her head, tutting her tongue. "How can you own a villa in Sardinia, and never want to play on the beach?"

"I'll play here," he said huskily, pulling her into his lap. "With you."

Her eyes widened, and Alessandro felt her instant surrender, her body's full attention. It was always like this between them. How many times had they made love since they'd wed? And yet he was still not satiated. He could not get enough of her.

Cupping her face, he pulled her mouth against his. Her lips felt so soft, so warm, and the stroke of her tongue felt like liquid fire. Her legs straddled his on the office chair, with her soft backside barely covered by the tiny bikini. The warmth between her legs pressed against the erection now straining beneath his trousers.

Kissing down her neck, he pressed his face between her large breasts, barely contained in the tiny triangles of fabric. She moaned as she moved against him, unconsciously grinding her body against him. He looked at her beautiful face. Her eyes were closed, her lips parted, her expression rapt. Even a lifetime wouldn't be enough to satisfy his endless desire for this incredible woman.

Twining a hand in her hair, he pulled down her head and gave her a hard, deep kiss as his other hand pulled the strings on her hips. Yanking off the bottom of her bikini, he tossed it to the floor and unzipped his fly, letting himself spring free. Lilley's eyes flew open as she realized what he intended, but it was too late.

Lifting her up, he brought her body down hard over him, impaling her in a single thrust. He groaned as he filled her so hard and deep that her body stiffened, even as she choked out a gasp of shock and pleasure.

He was deep inside her. Stretching her to the hilt. And it was good, so good. And wet. Oh God. Waves of sweet ecstasy washed over him and he closed his eyes. Lifting her a second time, he thrust again and a second, louder groan burst from his lips. But he didn't get the chance to do it again. She picked up the pace, her breasts swaying against his face as she controlled the rhythm. He leaned forward, breathing in the scent of sunshine and salt. Pushing aside a triangle of her bikini top, he suckled a swollen, taut nipple as his other hand gripped her thigh. She let out a little cry as she arched her body, tossing back her head as she rode him hard in his office chair, going faster, faster, deeper, deeper.

The pleasure was too intense. He hadn't taken her since

last night, which seemed like forever ago. His stamina wouldn't last. A low moan came from the back of her throat and he felt her soft breasts bounce against his mouth, felt her deep wet core sucking him further and further into ecstasy. He tried to restrain himself—to hold back the wave that threatened to burst. But he couldn't—hold back—for much longer—

Like a miracle, he heard a soft cry from her lips, which became louder as she clutched his shoulders with her hands, her fingernails gripping into his flesh. She gave a final sharp scream and he felt her convulse and tighten all around him. Just in time. In a rush, he surrendered to the pleasure and exploded into her. Lights danced behind his eyelids as he gave a ragged gasp, groaning as he pulsed and poured himself into her.

He held her for long moments in his office chair. When she finally rose unsteadily to her feet, he stood and zipped up his fly, still feeling disoriented. She was just wearing her bikini top and only half of that, really, since she had one breast exposed. He saw her shiver with cold and pulled off his long-sleeved, button-down shirt, wrapping it tenderly around her nearly naked body.

"Thanks," she murmured. She gave him a mischievous smile. "I love visiting you at work."

He laughed, then looked down at her. His tailored shirt hung down to her mid-thigh. "You look…cute."

"So do you." She ran her hand down his bare chest. "Because now you are far more suitably dressed…" She gave a sudden impish grin. "For the beach!"

He blinked at her.

"Woman!" he thundered. "When will you stop?"

"When you do what I want!"

"Not going to happen." He hesitated. "There's been a complication, Lilley. I need to leave for Rome."

"What's happened?"

He scowled. "Théo St. Raphaël happened."

She sucked in her breath. To his surprise, she seemed to understand the gravity of the situation even before he explained. "What—what about him?"

"It wasn't enough he stole the Joyería deal," he ground out. "Now he's after my expansion in Asia as well. Almost as if it's—personal."

"Maybe it is," she said in a small voice. "I don't get how you guys fight over things you don't even need. You have his winery. Call him. Offer an exchange. A truce—"

"Is that a joke?" he said in amazement. "I'd burn down my palazzo before I'd ask Théo St. Raphaël for a truce." He looked at her, and his voice gentled. "I am just sorry our honeymoon must end."

She licked her lips, then shrugged. "It's all right. I love Sardinia, but I'm sure I'll love Rome as well. I'm excited to see the palazzo. Meet your friends."

"Lilley." His good humor fled. "We've talked about this."

"*You've* talked about it," she said sulkily, her fingertips curling against the dark hair on his chest.

"You're my wife. You promised to obey me."

Indignant, she stared up at him. "I did no such—"

"Your place is at home," he interrupted.

"My home is with you." She looked down at her bare feet. "Unless you're ashamed of me."

Taking both her hands in his own, he pressed them to his lips. "My friends aren't the warmest, friendliest sort of people. I doubt you'd like them."

The cuffs of his long-sleeved shirt hung over her hands, making her look very young as she looked away. "You mean they won't like *me*."

"I'll send for you soon," he said softly, pulling her into his arms. "I promise." And to seal that vow, he lowered his mouth to hers in the gentlest, tenderest kiss he'd ever given her.

To his shock, she pulled away, her brown eyes flinty. "No."

His eyebrows lowered. "Don't you understand? I'm trying to protect you."

"I don't want to be protected, I want to be your wife!"

He exhaled, tried to keep his voice light. "If you're weary of Sardinia, I could leave you at our country estate in Tuscany. You could see the famous paintings of Florence, decorate the nursery, learn how to make bread—"

"No!" She stamped her foot against the marble floor, a gesture marred by the fact that she was barefoot and it caused a grimace of pain across her face. Rubbing the sole of her foot, she scowled at him. "I'm going with you to Rome!"

"Lilley," he tried, "please."

"I'm not afraid of your friends." When he didn't answer, she tossed her head. "What do you think they'll do? Fight me with their bare hands? Wrestle me into the mud?"

"No," he said quietly. "They'll be more subtle. They'll attack any weakness they can find. Your manners, your clothes, even your dyslexia—"

"Are you telling me," she said scornfully, "there'll be some kind of *reading test* before they let me in their little club?"

Trying to keep his patience, he set his jaw. "I am just trying to keep you happy and safe."

"By keeping me a prisoner?"

He folded his arms. "You're not exactly suffering here, Lilley. Most people would call this place heaven, not a prison." At her glare, he amended, "And it's just until your lessons are done. Until you're ready."

"So you *are* ashamed of me."

"Don't be ridiculous!"

"I won't embarrass you," she whispered. She looked up at him with pleading eyes, pressing her fingertips against his bare chest. "Please. Don't leave me here without you. I can't…I can't bear us to be apart."

He felt helpless against that gaze. Setting his jaw, he looked down at the floor. "They will hurt you."

"I'm stronger than you think."

"Olivia is there."

For a second, Lilley fell silent. Then she lifted her chin. "We'll have her to tea."

He snorted in disbelief. "That might be overdoing it."

"I'm serious," she insisted in a small voice. "I feel guilty. She was in love with you, she thought you were going to propose to her, and we eloped. We hurt her."

"*You* didn't do anything," he said sharply. "And if I treated her badly, she can handle it, believe me. She'll find someone else to marry, someone twice as rich and better-looking in the bargain."

"No one's better-looking than you," Lilley said, then her smile faded. She looked away, chewing on her bottom lip. "Do you think she was in love with you? Really and truly?"

Mesmerized, Alessandro watched her white teeth sinking into pink flesh that was full and swollen from days of lovemaking. Then he came back to himself. "Absolutely not," he said sharply. "She just knew as I did, that on paper, we were perfect for each other."

Lilley's expression fell, and it occurred to him that such an honest statement might hurt her feelings. "But now I have you," he said reassuringly. She blinked up at him. "The mother of my precious child," he added. Her lower lip wobbled. He wrapped his arm around her waist and said hopefully, "The woman who's given me the best sex of my life?"

A laugh finally escaped her. Then she shook her head, squaring her shoulders. "And I'm coming with you to Rome."

Alessandro's instincts screamed *No.* But he saw the yearning in her eyes and could not deny her what she wanted. What they both wanted. He didn't want to be apart from her, either.

"Very well, *cara,*" he said quietly. "Rome."

She sucked in her breath.

"Thank you!" she cried, flinging her arms around his shoulders. "You won't be sorry. You'll see. I can handle them. I'm not scared!"

As Lilley kissed his cheeks over and over, murmuring her appreciation, Alessandro almost believed he'd done the right thing. He would protect her, he told himself. And Lilley was strong. She'd gained a great deal of confidence in the days of their marriage. What had caused such a rapid change in her? The Italian lessons? The etiquette classes?

Whatever it was, she would be fine. He was worrying over nothing. After all, they were married now, and expecting a child. What on earth in Rome could possibly break them apart?

CHAPTER NINE

ROME. *Roma.* The Eternal City.

What was the Italian word for *disaster*?

Another fabulous, sophisticated dinner at an elegant restaurant with Alessandro's friends, and once again, Lilley was hiding in a bathroom stall. She was becoming a connoisseur of fancy Roman bathrooms.

Since they'd arrived in Rome three weeks ago, Alessandro had worked endless hours at the office. The only time she saw him—aside from the middle of the night when he made love to her—was at dinner, and that almost always included his friends, who were thrilled to see him.

They were not quite as thrilled about her.

For the last two hours, she'd sat at the table with a frozen smile on her face while Alessandro and his friends talked and laughed in rapid-fire Italian. And it was her own fault. But their first night in Rome, Alessandro had taken her to an elegant restaurant with an English menu. A kind gesture, but Lilley was so nervous, trying to make his glamorous friends like her, that the letters on the menus had refused to stay still. In the end, she'd tried to laugh it off, and her husband had taken over and gallantly ordered for her. But ever since, she'd insisted on only Italian menus. At least then she had an excuse for why she couldn't read them.

And she'd insisted to Alessandro that she preferred that

he speak to his friends in their native Italian. "I'll learn the language more quickly that way," she'd said.

What she'd mostly learned was that his friends made her uncomfortable and she wished that she and her husband could stay home. Home in the bedroom of their palazzo, where Alessandro made her so happy, or creating jewelry in her makeshift studio in the mews, or decorating the large sitting room she was turning into a nursery suite. Heck. Even going for another OB visit, with her chauffeur on one side and her bodyguard on the other, would be more fun than this.

Hiding in the bathroom stall, Lilley stared down at her beige Prada shoes. She'd lasted two hours before she fled to the bathroom. A new record, she tried to comfort herself. It was helpful to be pregnant, because no one questioned long disappearances. Lilley's beige designer suit skirt strained at the seams, feeling too tight around her waist, and she wished she hadn't eaten so much bread. None of the other women ate bread.

No. They seemed to survive on gossip and malice.

It's your imagination, she tried to tell herself. Her Italian was still pretty bad. Alessandro's friends could be saying anything, and she'd likely misread the women's sidelong glances. As soon as her language skills improved, she would no doubt discover his friends were actually quite nice....

The bathroom door banged open.

"Can you believe Alessandro is married to that fat pudding-faced creature who can barely read and has nothing to say for herself?"

Lilley froze, recognizing the voice.

"A tragedy," another woman agreed. "I can hardly believe a fine specimen like Alessandro was trapped by a stupid little nobody."

"Well. I wouldn't say she's *little,*" the first woman replied slyly.

Trembling, Lilley peeked through the crack in the stall door and saw Giulia and Lucretia standing at the wall of sleek sinks, refreshing their lipstick in the mirrors. Both of them wealthy heiresses married to still richer men. And they were both so thin they looked like clotheshangers in their designer clothes from Milan.

"Such a shame," Giulia sighed, giving her nose a pat of powder as she stared at herself in the mirror. "Olivia should be with us tonight, like always."

"She will be again," Lucretia said comfortingly. Smacking her lips together, she tucked her lipstick back into a tiny crystal clutch. "The fat little gold digger will realize she doesn't belong here. Once the brat is born, Alessandro will tire of her and send her back to America. Then he will be with Olivia again. As they were meant to be." She glanced at the other woman. "Are we done?"

"I think so," Giulia replied. Smiling at each other, they left the bathroom.

The bang of the door reverberated behind them. Lilley clasped her hands together, her heart pounding. Her skin felt clammy, her body flashing hot and cold. It was her own fault for remaining hidden, she told herself. If she'd come immediately out of the stall, Giulia and Lucretia would never have been so rude. They would not have been so cruel if they'd known she was there, listening.

Then Lilley realized—

The women had spoken in *English.*

"Oh," she breathed aloud, a soft gasp, falling back against the wall as if she'd been punched. Slowly, she swung open the stall door. She saw herself in the mirror, saw how little the stark, minimalist dress suited her taste or her figure. She was wearing the same style as Giulia and Lucretia, but instead of making her blend in with the fashionable set, it only emphasized the rounder shape of her body, and made her normally rosy skin seem washed-out and pale.

Or maybe their words had done that. Alessandro had said his friends could be mean, but she hadn't believed him. She'd never imagined anyone could be so deliberately cruel to a virtual stranger, a new bride far from her home country.

Lilley wondered what Giulia and Lucretia would say if they knew her father was Walton Hainsbury, if that would make her more palatable. But somehow she doubted it. They would simply find new reasons to mock her.

Staring at her own pale, miserable, and yes—a little pie-faced—expression, Lilley swallowed. The ache in her throat felt like a razor blade, but she wasn't going to show them they'd hurt her. No way. Straightening her shoulders, she went down the hall.

Her high-heeled shoes clicked against the floor as she walked across the elegant restaurant, past all the wealthy, gorgeous patrons who actually looked as if they fitted in here. She saw Alessandro sitting beside Giulia and Lucretia and their husbands, tossing his head back in laughter as the women regarded him with sharp, sly smiles. And suddenly, Lilley's courage failed her. Turning, she veered towards the bar.

A handsome young bartender in a white jacket, drying glasses with a white towel, turned to her. *"Sì, signorina?"*

Lilley looked at the wall of liquor bottles behind the bar. If ever a moment called for liquid courage, this was it. But she was pregnant, and anyway she'd never had much experience with alcohol. Except for the night of the Preziosi di Caetani ball, when she'd drunk a glass and a half of champagne. Alessandro had made her feel so precious and beautiful… Her eyes filled with tears.

"Signorina?" the bartender said. *"Prende qualcosa?"*

She wiped her eyes. *"Acqua frizzante, per favore."*

A large hand grabbed her shoulder. With an intake of breath, she turned, but it wasn't Alessandro. Instead, she saw a dark man with ice-blue eyes, an acquaintance of her husband's that she'd met at a cocktail party a few nights before. The Russian tycoon who owned gold mines across the Yukon…what was his name? "Prince Vladimir. Hello."

The man looked down at her with interest. "What are you doing here, little one?" He looked around. "Where is your husband? You do not look well."

"I'm fine. Great in fact." Blinking back tears, she turned back to the bartender as he held out her sparkling water. "Oh no—I forgot my purse!"

"Please. Allow me," Prince Vladimir said, pulling out his wallet. He blinked with surprise when the bartender told him the amount. "So little?"

"It's water," Lilley said. "I'm pregnant."

"Ah," Prince Vladimir said. "Congratulations."

"Thank you. Not everyone knows yet." Lilley glanced back at the table across the room. "Believe me, if I could drink something stronger, I would."

Vladimir followed her glance, and understanding filled his eyes. "Ah. But you have nothing to fear, *Principessa,*" he said quietly. "Your husband is smitten. I've seen the way he looks at you."

Holding the cold glass against the hot skin of her cheek, she whispered, "You mean the way he doesn't look at me."

"Then he is a fool." He put his finger on her bulky crystal necklace. "This is beautiful. Where did you buy it?"

Startled by his touch, Lilley nearly jumped. "I made it."

"You did!"

She shook her head. "Alessandro doesn't want me to wear it in Rome. He said it might make his friends laugh at me, but I don't care. They're going to laugh anyway," she said in a low voice. She straightened. "I have to wear one thing that feels like mine."

"It's beautiful." His finger ran along the bottom edge of her necklace, just below her collarbone. "It's art."

His touch made her uncomfortable. Innocent as it was, the situation might be misconstrued. Even now, Alessandro might be watching them, growing wild with jealousy…

She glanced back at their table, and saw he was busy laughing, having the time of his life with his cold-hearted friends, saying things she couldn't remotely understand.

Clearly, Lilley's plan to make Alessandro fall wildly in love with her was going perfectly.

Tears filled her eyes. How she wished they were still in Sardinia, with nothing but warm sunlight, cool blue water and swaying palm trees around them, far from the rest of the world!

Instead, she was here with him in Rome. As she'd insisted. And as he'd warned her, she was miserable.

Vladimir followed her gaze. "Come, *Principessa,*" he said quietly. "I will take you back to him."

As he led her across the elegant restaurant, the tension in Lilley's throat ratcheted up with every step. They reached the table, and the laughter of the group abruptly fell silent.

"Cara." Alessandro turned with a smile. "I was starting to wonder…" Then he saw Vladimir behind her, and the tenderness in his eyes evaporated. He said shortly, "Hello."

"Your wife isn't feeling well," Prince Vladimir said. "I suggest you take her home."

"Yes," Alessandro said grimly, rising to his feet. Throwing money on the table, he said to his friends, *"Mi scusi. Buona notte."*

Placing his hand against the small of Lilley's back, Alessandro escorted her out of the restaurant. Collecting his Ferrari from the valet, he helped her into the car. He didn't speak. He didn't even look at her.

He drove swiftly and silently through the streets of Rome, and Lilley glanced at him out of the corner of her eye. His face was dark, his expression hard. Miserably, she looked away.

The harder she tried to please him, she thought in despair, the worse it seemed to get.

"I'm sorry," she whispered. "I didn't mean for you to have to leave your friends early."

Alessandro changed the gears on the Ferrari with more force than necessary. His jaw was tense as he said in a low voice, "I'm sorry you felt it necessary to tell Vladimir Xendzov you wished to leave, rather than coming to me."

She blinked at him. "I was just trying to—"

"Save it," he cut her off. He pulled past the guardhouse outside their palazzo, driving through the gate.

Parking his car haphazardly in the small courtyard, he stomped into the sixteenth-century palace. Hurt and furious, Lilley followed him. He was far ahead of her, already halfway up the dark, sweeping stairs, when she stopped, clenching her hands.

"You're not being fair!" she bit out.

Alessandro stopped on the stairs, pulling off his tie. He looked down at her, his jaw set. "Are you coming to bed?"

Lilley blinked, taken aback. He stood above her, his button-down shirt tight across his muscular chest, his black trousers fitted low on his hips. Yes. She wanted to go to bed with Alessandro, damn him. Angry as she was, her nipples were hard, her breasts heavy and she felt a spiraling need low and deep in her belly. Her body was instantly at his command.

But—make love with a cold heart? When they both were angry?

She straightened, tightening her hands, and vehemently shook her head.

"I *said,*" his voice was deceptively cold as he came down the steps towards her, "are you coming to bed?"

"No," she ground out.

His black eyes glittered.

"Then," he said, "I will bring bed to you."

She saw the intent in his eyes the instant before he grabbed her. Cupping the back of her head, he lowered his mouth to hers in a punishing kiss. As she tried to push him away, his hands gripped her hair, and he deepened the kiss, wrenching her lips apart with his own. He used his tongue like a sensual weapon, plundering her mouth, and, against her will, her body responded. As her sensitive nipples brushed against him, her breasts were crushed against his hard chest, and she melted into his arms.

Leaning her back against the stairs, he kissed her with such brutal ferocity that she surrendered, allowing him to push her down onto the carpet. With a low growl, he yanked her skirt up to her hips. Without a word, he started to unzip his fly.

That woke her up.

"No," she said, grabbing his wrist as she looked straight into his eyes. "No."

His eyes widened. He exhaled, then pulled away. Rising to his feet, he zipped up his trousers, not looking at her.

"I never want to see you with Vladimir Xendzov again," he said coldly. Then, without a look, he walked up the stairs.

Lilley sat up, feeling disheveled and dizzy, her skirt at her waist. He'd nearly made love to her—and she'd nearly let him do it! Then, when she'd refused him, he'd just left her! Her fury returned, redoubled. Standing up, she readjusted her ugly, expensive beige skirt. Her eyes narrowed as she followed him up the stairs to their bedroom, where she heard the shower running in the en suite bathroom. She pushed open the door, and saw him in the shower, standing naked beneath the running water.

Yanking open the glass door, she leaned into the shower and slammed on the handle, shutting off his water.

"What the hell?" he exploded.

Hot steam floated between them, water dripping noisily off the travertine wall. She glared at him, folding her arms. "How dare you treat me like that, you big—jerk!"

"What did you expect?" he ground out. "That I'd kiss your toes with adoration after you spent the whole night flirting with another man?"

"I wasn't flirting! He was comforting me! After—"

Alessandro's eyes narrowed. "After what?"

She swallowed, fighting tears. "It doesn't matter."

He stepped out of the shower, his body naked and dripping wet. His voice was dangerous as he said, "Tell me."

In the mirror, she saw the reflection of his magnificent, naked body, and next to him, she saw herself, fat and dowdy in the unflattering beige suit that made her look like a lump. "I can't."

"Tell me!" he thundered.

She flinched, and her lips turned down. "They were mean to me."

He gripped the door of the shower. "Who? Who was mean to you?"

"You were right," Lilley whispered. "I never should have come to Rome." She blinked back tears. "I don't belong here."

Moving forward, Alessandro grabbed her shoulders. His eyes were dark as he said in a low voice, "Just tell me who."

She tried to laugh it off. "Nothing, really. They followed me into the bathroom where I was hiding at the restaurant—"

"You were hiding?"

"—and spoke to each other. In English, to be sure I'd understand. They called me fat and stupid, and said you'd divorce me. They couldn't wait for you to be back with Olivia."

He stared at her, his mouth a grim line. Then he abruptly released her, turning away. Lilley stared at his muscular backside as he headed for the door.

He was walking away from her without a word. Again.

"Don't you care?" she choked out. "Don't you care at all?"

Alessandro whirled around, and his expression was so full of fury that she gasped.

"I care," he said. "They will regret hurting you."

"What are you going to do?" she whispered, afraid of the strange darkness she saw in his eyes.

"They are women. I cannot physically hurt them. But," he stretched his intertwined hands, "I can take what they care about the most. Their money."

"How?"

He looked past her ear. "A few well-placed calls to the banks…to the businesses that employ their husbands in well-paid sinecures." He gave a smile as cold as death. "They'll be penniless."

She stared at him, her mouth agape. "I thought they were rich."

"It's a front. They're deeply in debt."

"I thought they were your friends!"

His lip twisted. "Friends?"

"You seemed to be having such a good time…"

"I grew up with them," he said tersely. "But we're not close. We share a past. We share a history. But no. They are not my friends."

Staring up at him, Lilley thought of the friends she'd had

in Minnesota growing up, playing marbles with the housekeeper's daughter Lisa, going for long bike rides with Katie from school, ice skating on the pond with her friends and drinking hot chocolate.

Alessandro hadn't had that. His friends weren't real. Pity and grief for him welled up inside her. And suddenly she couldn't hide her feelings. Not any more.

"I don't need revenge." Blinking back tears, she took a step towards him. "There's only one thing I want. One thing I need."

His jaw twitched. "What?"

"You," she whispered. "I love you, Alessandro."

She heard the catch of his breath. Then his eyes became wistful.

"I know," he said quietly. "I've known since before our wedding, when you almost blurted it out, and I stopped you."

"What?" She didn't remember anything like that. "What are you talking about?"

"Don't you remember? You said you had something to tell me before we could marry. I stopped you because I already knew. You were in love with me. I could see your feelings on your face."

Lilley's lips parted as she remembered the moment in Las Vegas when she'd tried to tell him the truth about her family. "That was what you thought I was going to say?" she said slowly. "That I was in love with you?"

He shook his head. "I couldn't let you speak the words. I thought it would ruin things between us, that it would make a good marriage impossible."

He didn't know. Lilley's head was spinning. Alessandro didn't know about her family. All these weeks they'd been married, she'd thought he was so kind not to reproach her, so generous to forgive and forget. But he hadn't known. He still didn't know!

"But now," Alessandro said in a low voice, "I don't know what to think. I don't know if I can love anyone, Lilley." Clenching his jaw, he looked away. "When I was nineteen, I was betrayed by everyone who loved me. The woman I thought I loved told me she was pregnant by another man. My father died after ignoring me most of his life. And then my mother," he took a deep breath, "informed me that I was not his son."

"What?" Lilley gasped.

"By their second year of marriage, she'd already grown to hate him. She had a brief affair, and got pregnant with me. My father never knew. He died thinking I was his son, and still left me nothing but debts and an unknown number of half-brothers and half-sisters around the world."

Grief was shining in his black eyes. She'd never seen him so open with his feelings before. "I'm sorry," she choked out, wrapping her arms around him. "Who is your real father?"

He looked away. "Not someone I ever wanted to know."

"I'm sorry," she breathed again, but it seemed woefully inadequate. Reaching up, she kissed his cheeks, his lips, his chin, his shoulders. She offered comfort by kissing every part of him she could reach. "I'm so sorry." Tears streamed unchecked down her face as their eyes met. "But I'm your family now."

He exhaled as he looked down at her. "I don't know if I can love you, Lilley," he said in a low voice. His dark eyes shimmered. "But if I could ever love any woman on earth… it would be you."

Lilley's heart stopped beating, then suddenly raced at a gallop. "It would?"

"You're the first woman I've trusted in a long, long time,"

he said softly, stroking her cheek. "Because I know you'd never lie to me—about anything."

A tremble went through her. How could she ever tell him about her family now? How could she possibly explain what had started as a fib of omission to help her get a job, but had turned into months of lying straight to his face?

Honey, she could say casually over waffles some Sunday, *a funny thing about how you thought my father owned a shop. He does own a store, but a few more than one!* Maybe they'd have a good laugh. Maybe he'd forgive her.

But then she'd have to tell him about Théo.

She had to tell him. Before he found out some other way. And she would, she promised herself. Once their marriage was on stronger footing. Once his friends didn't hate her. Then she would tell him everything. She *would.* Even though it would make him hate her.

She trembled just to think of it....

"I'm sorry I never gave you the wedding you deserved," Alessandro said, stroking her cheek.

She gasped. "I loved our wedding!"

He shook his head ruefully. "You should have had friends at the ceremony. Family." He looked at her. "Have you told your father about me yet?"

Her father. She swallowed. "Um. No. Not yet." Squaring her shoulders, she forced herself to add, "But I will take you to Minnesota to meet him. Anytime you like."

"How about Christmas?" Holding her in his arms, he smiled down at her, the expression on his handsome face tender and bright. "We'll have a wedding reception in Rome first. Then plan one there."

"A reception?"

"Two. One on each continent. I want to properly celebrate." He stroked her hair. "With our family and friends."

"Oh," she breathed.

"It'll give your father a chance to know me." He gave her a sudden wink. "I'll win him over."

His charm and thoughtfulness just made her feel more guilty. "Of course you will," she said over the lump in her throat. "No one could help loving you."

His expression grew serious. "But I don't need anyone to love me." He pulled her against his naked body, stroking her back over her beige jacket. "I only need you."

Lilley suddenly felt like crying. She felt his naked body stir, and her own immediate response flooded her with need. She shivered as his hands gently caressed her breasts over the fabric, squeezing her plump flesh with his fingers, rubbing her swollen nipples until they were hard and aching beneath her jacket.

Her gaze fell on the bathroom mirrors and she saw their image, his naked body and muscular backside, as his lips lowered to her neck. The image caused a wave of immediate pleasure as he unbuttoned her jacket.

"You're mine," he murmured against her skin. She felt him hard between her legs, felt the gentle, insistent stroke of his fingertips as he pulled off her silk camisole and bra, running his palm down the valley between her pregnant breasts to her small waist and softly rounded belly. "Say it."

She opened her eyes. "I'm yours."

"Forever," he demanded.

She swallowed. "Forever."

Alessandro fell to his knees in front of her. Lifting her skirt to her hips, he yanked her panties to the floor. Moving his head between her thighs, he lifted one of her legs over his shoulder.

Her hands gripped his naked, hard-muscled shoulders as she felt his hot breath between her thighs. Then, the last moment before he kissed her, he lifted his head to look at her face.

"Never lie to me, Lilley," he whispered. "And we'll last forever. No one will ever be able to break us apart."

He lowered his mouth between her legs, and as waves of pleasure exploded inside her, Lilley tilted back her head with a gasp, closing her eyes. Her heart pounded as she realized what she'd done. She should have told him the truth from the beginning. From the very first day. She'd thought it would be better to wait until he had a reason to care. But when he discovered she'd lied to him for months, after he'd allowed himself to be so vulnerable and care for her—trust her—it would be the beginning of the end.

No. She felt his wet, slick tongue between her legs and shuddered with need, closing her eyes with anguish. She couldn't lose him. Not now. Not ever.

She would find a way to tell him the truth. And pray it wasn't the end…of everything.

CHAPTER TEN

ALESSANDRO's jaw dropped when he first saw his wife at the top of the stairs.

After five weeks of planning, he'd known she was choosing her gown with care for their wedding reception at their palazzo tonight. She'd insisted on picking her dress herself, in utmost secrecy. Now he saw why. Lilley was wearing a ball gown of watered silk in blending swirls of purple and fuchsia, with a snug corset tight beneath her breasts and loose over her swelling belly. Pink flowers adorned her long, flowing brown hair which tumbled over her shoulders.

She paused at the top of the landing, waiting for his reaction. "Well?" she asked with a deep breath. "What do you think?"

Alessandro opened his lips to tell her she must change, to tell her she couldn't wear such an outrageous gown, not when they'd be surrounded by the critical eyes of the most stylish citizens of the most stylish city in the world. He opened his mouth to tell her that fitting in was the only way to survive.

Then Alessandro saw the hope in Lilley's vulnerable brown eyes. He realized what a risk she'd taken, choosing a dress like this for the night of the reception she'd spent weeks planning.

She was, quite deliberately, taking a risk.

And the truth was she looked beautiful. Looking at her face, Alessandro suddenly didn't give a damn what anyone else thought. He didn't care about anyone but her.

He held up his hand with a smile. "You look beautiful."

Relief and gratitude rushed across Lilley's beautiful face before she gave him a mischievous grin. *"Grazie,"* she said, swishing her skirt as she came down the stairs. She adjusted his tie with a dimpled smile. "You don't look so bad in that tuxedo yourself."

Then, standing on her tiptoes, she reached up and kissed him so long and hard that if guests for the reception hadn't already started to arrive, he would have taken her straight upstairs and ripped the colorful ball gown right off her.

As they went to the ballroom to greet their guests, Alessandro marveled at the changes Lilley had made in the palazzo. In the two months they'd been in Rome, Lilley had tossed out all his elegant, creaky antiques and replaced them with furniture that was both comfortable and warm. His palazzo had once been a showplace. Now it was a home.

And it had never looked better than it did tonight. It was early December, and there was a fire in every fireplace, white twinkling lights on the trees outside and holly and pine boughs on all the mantels, to celebrate the upcoming season.

Looking across the ballroom, Lilley gave a sudden intake of breath. "Uh-oh. The ambassador is hitting on Monica Valenti." He followed her gaze to see the gray-haired ambassador clearly invading the personal space of the nineteen-year-old starlet. Lilley threw him an apologetic glance. *"Mi scusi."*

As he took a flute of champagne from a passing waiter, Alessandro watched his wife with admiration. Their ballroom was packed. Lilley had invited everyone: aristocracy, government officials and entrepreneurs, from the highest circles of Roman society. She'd even invited Lucretia and Giulia.

His wife had a forgiving soul. He did not.

Alessandro had called both women and disinvited them in no uncertain terms. Now they were missing this reception, which somehow—he wasn't sure quite how—had turned into the social event of the year. The humiliation would teach the two women to show his wife a little more respect. His lips curled. The next time Lilley saw them, he suspected they would be in a far friendlier mood.

Finishing the glass of St. Raphaël champagne, he placed his empty flute on a silver tray and watched as his beautiful wife disengaged Monica Valenti from the ambassador with such friendly, warm charm, that instead of taking offense, the gray-haired man smiled at her, clearly enchanted.

And who wouldn't be enchanted? Surrounded by skinny women who wore drab designer gowns of beige and black, Lilley stood out like a bird of paradise. Guests followed her, waiting to speak with her, and Alessandro suddenly remembered how shy and terrified Lilley had been when he'd taken her to the Preziosi di Caetani ball. That was just a few months ago. So much had changed since then.

Lilley's eyes met his across the crowded ballroom, and he gave her a wicked half smile, thinking of what he intended to do to her later. Her brown eyes widened, and her cheeks turned a charming shade of pink. Ah, she was so adorable, his wife. So innocent and easy to read.

She looked away, their eye contact broken as a man came to speak with her, blocking Alessandro's view of her face.

He scowled as he recognized Vladimir Xendzov talking to Lilley, touching the bulky necklace around her neck. It was her newest strange concoction, created from gold and sapphire gem clusters she'd found in an antique shop in Venice. He wondered what they were talking about. He trusted his wife, but he didn't trust Xendzov. Setting his jaw, he grabbed a glass of bubbly pink champagne, then gaped at the raspberry in the bottom. He'd look like a fool drinking *that.* Setting the flute back on the tray, he barked at the waiter, "Get me a Scotch."

The man bowed and backed away, and Alessandro looked slowly around the crowded ballroom. Lilley had thrown herself into planning this reception as if her life depended on it, finding caterers and musicians and florists. The end result was as unique and offbeat as Lilley's jewelry. No one was dancing yet, but the mood was lively with a brash, lilting Irish rock band Lilley had hired from Dublin, just for fun. Dinner was being served buffet-style, with exotic dishes representing every country where Caetani Worldwide owned a subsidiary. The hodgepodge of cultures should have been a disaster. Instead… He looked around and saw powerful men laughing, saw their beige-clad wives giggling like schoolchildren. It was a hit.

Lilley was a hit.

Emotion rose in Alessandro's heart.

Why had he never realized it before? Lilley was perfect as she was. She didn't need to change. She didn't need to fit in. She was born to stand out.

The feeling in his heart expanded to his throat, choking him, and suddenly he had to tell her. He had to take her in his arms and tell her how proud he was of her, how much he cared about her, how much he…that he…

His feet moved across the marble floor, beneath the twinkling lights of the multicolored, sparkling glass chandeliers she'd bought in Venice. Alessandro moved faster, pushing through the crowds. His view of Lilley's face was still blocked by the people clustered around her, by the Russian who called himself a *prince.* Alessandro needed his wife in his arms. Now.

"Darling." Olivia suddenly stood in front of him, blocking his way. Skinny and pale, dressed in a black sheath that showed her complete lack of décolletage, she looked like an angel of death.

"What are you doing here?" he demanded.

"I was invited." Her lips curled up on the edges, reminding him of a cat, although that seemed disrespectful to cats. "By your *wife*."

She spoke the word as if it left her mouth with a foul taste. He set his jaw, glaring at her. "Lilley is too generous."

"Of course she is generous," Olivia's smile widened. "She can afford to be."

"What are you talking about?"

"She's rich."

Alessandro snorted. "Lilley doesn't come from money. That's one of the things that makes her so trustworthy. So different from you," he said pointedly.

She gave a tinkling little laugh. "Oh, this is delicious. Do you truly not know?" She walked slowly around him, running one red-painted fingertip along the shoulder of his tuxedo jacket. Her thin face was smug as she leaned forward to whisper, "She's Walton Hainsbury's daughter."

Alessandro stared at her. As if from a distance, he heard the lilting rock music, heard the laughter and low conversation of the Italian guests around him, the crème de la crème of Roman society. Then the marble floor seemed to move beneath his feet.

Walton Hainsbury's daughter. The man who owned the huge discount jewelry chain that had tried to seize control of Caetani Worldwide in a hostile takeover last spring. He shook his head fiercely.

"You're insane," Alessandro said. "Lilley comes from a little town in the midwest."

Olivia threw back her head and laughed. "You mean

Minneapolis? Oh, darling." She made a show of wiping her eyes. "It's a large city. The headquarters of many international corporations." She lifted a perfectly groomed eyebrow. "Including..."

Including Hainsbury Corporation, he remembered with a sickening twist of his gut. And Walton Hainsbury lived nearby. An icy chill went down his spine. He lifted his chin. "Lilley is not his daughter."

"Not just a daughter, but his only child. His heir."

My father threatened to disinherit me, her voice whirled through Alessandro's brain, *if I didn't come back to Minnesota and marry one of his managers.*

She'd had that platinum Hainsbury watch, which her mother had had especially made. How? How had she done that?

My father's a businessman.

He owns a restaurant? Perhaps a laundromat?

Um. Something like that.

Alessandro ignored the sudden pounding of his heart. He wouldn't believe it. He couldn't. "When we met, Lilley was working in my file room. My *file room,* Olivia."

She looked down at her finely sharpened red fingernails. "What better place for a corporate spy?"

A strangled noise escaped Alessandro's throat. He remembered finding Lilley alone in his private office that first night. *I just wanted to work for a few hours in peace and quiet. Without anyone bothering me,* she'd said.

His throat closed. And most damning of all. She'd known. She'd known about his plans for the Joyería deal. She could have given that information to Théo St. Raphaël.

Impossible, he told himself harshly. Lilley had no connection to the French count. Perhaps she'd had a motive to hate Alessandro back then, after he'd seduced and abandoned her in Sonoma. But she'd had no opportunity to...

"I'm surprised your company even hired her," Olivia said thoughtfully. "Considering her last employer."

Alessandro tried to remember the job Lilley had mentioned, the most recent one, which for some reason she'd left off her résumé. It all seemed like a million years ago. "She worked as a maid. In Minneapolis. And she worked for a relative…"

She looked at him in disbelief. "I've never seen you so stupid and slow. Until six months ago, she was Théo St. Raphaël's housekeeper in the South of France. He's her cousin, you know. She left his employ just days before she started working for you."

It felt like getting hit in the face. Alessandro staggered back. "Théo St. Raphaël?" he said faintly. "The Count of Castelnau is Lilley's cousin?"

"She's lied to you all along." Olivia regarded him. "But you expected that, didn't you? You always expect women to lie to you. Surely you had her background checked before you married her?"

His heart hammered in his chest, so hard and fast he thought it might break through his ribs. "No."

"Prenup?"

The ballroom, the noise of the guests, seemed to be spinning around him. The crowds parted, and he saw Lilley's face. She smiled at him across the room, her face shining, as honest and bright and beautiful as ever. He turned his head away, feeling sick. "No."

"Clever girl," Olivia murmured. "I wonder what else she's lied to you about." She gave him a sideways glance. "How well do you really know her?"

His jaw was tight. "I know she's pregnant with my child."

"Do you?" Her eyes were steady and cold. "Do you really?"

It felt like an ice pick through Alessandro's brain. He

heard the echo of Heather's voice from long ago. *The baby's not yours. I lied.*

He tightened his hands to fists. "Of course the baby is mine," he ground out. "Lilley wouldn't lie about that."

"You know how conniving and ruthless people can be."

"I know how conniving *you* can be," he said harshly.

"Me? I'm an amateur." Olivia laughed, covering her mouth with her hand. "All this time you believed her to be some small-town innocent, didn't you? And she probably planned this from the start. Perhaps her goal is full control of Caetani Worldwide, split equally between her father and her cousin."

He stared at her. "I don't believe you," he choked out.

But that was a lie. He did believe her. That was the problem.

Olivia's eyes met his. "So ask her."

With a low curse, Alessandro pushed past her. Shoving through the crowd, Alessandro stalked towards his wife. Just moments before, he'd felt such reckless joy, a strange breathless certainty about Lilley. Now, that feeling had evaporated as if it had never existed. All that was left was cold despair.

And fury. As he walked towards her, blood started to pound through his body, boiling hot, thawing him out limb by limb. He welcomed the anger. Stoked it.

He'd given Lilley everything, and she'd made a fool out of him. She'd lied to him from the beginning. Faked her name. Her résumé. And perhaps even—

No. He cut off the thought savagely, his hands clenching at his sides. Guests saw his face and backed away, the crowd parting for him like magic.

Lilley was laughing as she talked to Vladimir Xendzov, and the man's eyes caressed her face with admiration. Was

Lilley flirting with him? Toying with him? Using him, as she'd used Alessandro?

Lilley looked over Xendzov's shoulder and blanched when she saw Alessandro. "What's happened?" she breathed. "What's wrong?"

"Tell me your name," Alessandro said in a low voice.

The other guests clustered around Lilley glanced between them, suddenly uneasy at his tone of voice. Looking bewildered, she answered, "Lilley Caetani."

"No." He set his jaw, hating her soft, deceptive beauty that had lured him into trusting her. And more. "Tell me your *name*."

More guests fell silent, turning to look. The Irish rock music abruptly stopped. Suddenly, amid hundreds of people, it was quiet.

His wife swallowed, looking to the right and left. Then with a deep breath, she whispered, "Lilley Smith."

"Tell me!" He thundered. "Your *name!*"

She suddenly looked as if she was going to cry. "Alessandro, I was going to tell you."

"When?" he bit out. "After you'd stolen my company for Hainsbury and your cousin to pick through?"

"No!" she gasped. "I tried to tell you before our wedding. You said you already knew. You always know so much. I believed you!"

"You believed I would actually marry you, knowing that? You lied from the start, even about your name!"

She flinched. He saw the tremble of her eyelashes. "I changed my name three years ago, when my father divorced my mother while she was dying. I didn't want to be a Hainsbury anymore. So I took her maiden name—"

"You knew Caetani Worldwide would never hire you with either Hainsbury or Théo St. Raphaël's name on your résumé."

"Yes," she admitted in a small voice.

"You came as a spy."

"No! I was just desperate for a job while I tried to start my business!" She shook her head tearfully. "I went to San Francisco to follow my dream—"

"Bull," he said brutally. "You went to San Francisco to seduce Jeremy Wakefield into giving you information about Preziosi designs, so your father could have them copied in China in advance. Until I took you to the Preziosi ball and you realized a greater prize was possible for you." He gave a hard laugh. "You decided to become my mistress, so you could funnel information to your family."

"I would never betray you!" she said with a sob. "I was going to tell you everything! I swore it to myself, when I finally realized you didn't know about my family. All this time, I thought you did, until the day I first told you I loved you."

Her voice trembled, but her tears weren't going to work on him, not this time. "That was weeks ago." He grabbed her by the shoulders, looking fiercely into her weepy eyes. "All this time, I thought I could trust you. And you were waiting to stab me in the back. What was your goal? How are they going to work against me? Are your father and cousin planning a hostile takeover of my company?"

"You know me better than that!" She hiccupped, and her eyes became huge as she looked up at him. Unchecked tears streaked her rosy cheeks as she whispered, "Don't you?"

"I wish to God I'd never met you." Alessandro's pulse hammered in his ears, and he couldn't breathe. Couldn't even think. "There's just one last thing I need to know."

"What?"

He gently touched her full bottom lip, the lip he'd once thought could only speak the truth. "How deep do your lies go?"

Her lips parted beneath his touch. His hand slowly traced down her neck, skimming over the breasts and corset to the bright pink-and-purple skirts that covered her swollen belly. "Is the baby mine?"

Her eyes widened as she gasped.

"Tell me the truth, Lilley," he said in a low, dangerous voice. "Did you sleep with another man?"

A sob came from the back of her throat. As he stared down at Lilley's beautiful, tortured face, Alessandro suddenly forgot about the crowded ballroom, forgot Caetani Worldwide, forgot Olivia behind him. All he could think was that he'd loved Lilley. That had been the feeling swelling in his heart moments before. That had been what he'd wanted to tell her. *He loved her.*

But now he knew the woman he'd loved was a lie. Lilley had deceived him from the beginning. He'd asked for a paternity test, and she'd talked him out of it. She'd lured him into loving her, so she could rip out his heart. Just like all the rest.

Unwilling memories rushed through him. Lilley's teasing smile as she tried to get him to play. Lilley naked in the pool in Sardinia. Lilley defending everyone, even people who didn't deserve it. Lilley clinging to him for comfort and strength. Lilley's deep, loving eyes that promised eternity. All a lie.

She stood in front of him now, swaying on her feet, looking as if she might faint. "You really think I would do that?" she whispered. "That I'd sleep with another man, then marry you and spend the rest of my life lying to you? How can you think that? I love you!"

"Nice," he murmured. Touching her cheek, he tilted her face towards the light of the chandelier. "The tears in your eyes, the catch in your voice." He dropped his hand and said acidly, "You'd almost have me believe that you cared."

"I do care!" she choked out. "I love you—"

"Stop saying that," he said harshly, then set his jaw, glaring at her with hatred. "Fine. Don't tell me. I wouldn't believe a word you said anyway."

Lilley clasped her hands together, looking pale and small in her vivid ball gown, flowers tumbling from her long brown hair. Then she glanced at Olivia behind him.

"She did this, didn't she? She took my white lie and twisted it into evidence of a black heart." A tremble filled her voice as she looked back at him. Tears were streaking her face. "And you believed her. You never thought I was good enough to be your wife. You never wanted to love me. And this is your easy way out."

"I despise you," he said coldly.

She gave a sob, and Vladimir Xendzov placed a hand on his shoulder. "Enough. You've made your point."

Alessandro twisted out of the man's grasp, barely restraining himself from punching his face. "Stay out of this." He suddenly hated Xendzov, Olivia and every other vulture in his colorful, festive ballroom. Setting his jaw, he looked around the ballroom and shouted, "All of you—get the hell out!"

"No," Lilley said behind him. "Stop it, Alessandro."

Her voice was harder and colder than he'd ever heard from her lips before. Surprised, he turned back to face her.

Lilley's eyes were still grief-stricken but her shoulders were straight, her body rigid. "Our guests haven't done anything to deserve your abuse. And neither have I." She squared her shoulders and said, "Either tell me, *right now,* that you know this baby is yours, or I will leave you. And never come back."

An ultimatum. He stiffened. "I'm just supposed to trust your word, am I?"

Lilley's face turned pale, almost gray. "I'm not going to

stay in a marriage you don't know how to fight for." She glanced back at Olivia bitterly. "She's the one you always wanted. A woman as perfect and heartless as you."

In a swirl of purple-and-pink skirts, Lilley turned away.

Alessandro grabbed her shoulder. "You can't leave," he ground out. "Not without a paternity test."

She looked at him, and he could have drowned in the deep grief of her brown eyes. "I'm done trying to make you love me," she whispered. "Done."

Alessandro couldn't show weakness. Couldn't let her know how close she'd come to breaking him entirely. "You'll stay in Rome," he said harshly. "Until I allow you to leave."

Her eyes glittered.

"No," she said. "I won't."

Her face looked strange, her eyes half-wild as she took a deep breath.

"I slept with a different man, just like you said." Blinking back tears as she looked up at him, she choked out with a sob, "And I loved him."

Her words were like a serrated blade across Alessandro's heart. He staggered back, stricken. "And the baby," he breathed, searching her eyes. "What about the baby?"

Lilley's brown eyes were dark as a winter storm. Tears streamed down her face like rain. For answer, she pulled her canary-yellow diamond ring off her left hand and wordlessly held it out to him.

Numbly, he reached for it. Lilley turned away, pushing through the crowds, not looking back.

And this time, he didn't try to stop her. Gripping the ten-carat diamond ring tightly against his palm, Alessandro closed his eyes, leaning his head against his fist as he felt the first spasms of grief course through his body.

CHAPTER ELEVEN

A WEEK later, Alessandro sat in his study staring at divorce papers, feeling numb.

He hadn't seen Lilley since she'd fled the reception, running out into the streets of Rome with only her passport and wallet, still dressed in the fuchsia ball gown. He had no idea where she was, and didn't care. Let the lawyers find her.

He looked down wearily at the documents spread across his desk. He didn't need Lilley, he told himself. He didn't need their baby.

Except a hard lump rose in his throat every time he passed the room that would have been the nursery. The walls were soft yellow, and Lilley's painting of baby elephants, monkeys and giraffes was propped against the wall. Alessandro's car still held the stuffed elephant he'd bought the day before the reception, and it was in his trunk right now, wrapped in festive paper decorated with baby animals, tied with a bright yellow bow.

The ache in his throat increased. Alessandro clenched his jaw. He'd burn the toy, he thought savagely. Then he'd repaint the nursery's walls with a color that wouldn't remind him of either Lilley or the baby. No blue. No pink. He couldn't use brown, either, the color of her eyes. Nor red, the color of her lips. So what was left?

Black. Just black.

He leaned his forehead into his hands. He was better off without them. Better off without Lilley constantly pestering him to jump in the pool or dance or play. Without hearing her soft voice speak dreamily of their future children, of a happy marriage that would last fifty years. Without seeing the sensual, breathless expression in her face as she looked up at him in bed, the moment before he pushed inside her.

Va bene. He didn't need them. He'd go back to the life he'd had before, working all day to earn money he didn't need, having meaningless affairs that were forgotten by morning. Trusting no one. Forever alone. *Perfetto.*

He covered his face with his hands.

His phone rang. "*Buon giorno,* darling," Olivia said cheerfully. "Now you're rid of your mistake, I want to ask you to lunch. To celebrate."

"I'm not divorced yet," he said in a low voice.

"Come to lunch anyway. I don't mind."

Her low, smug voice jarred him. Swiveling in his chair, he turned towards the window, towards the view of the city and hazy blue sky. Where was Lilley? Was she with another man? He remembered the way Vladimir Xendzov had looked at her. Remembered Jeremy Wakefield's awed face when he saw her in the red dress.

Who was the father of her baby?

I slept with a different man, just like you said. And I loved him.

His lips twisted. That meant she'd lied when she'd told Alessandro she loved *him.* Another lie to add to the pile.

Through the window, he saw a limo park at the gate of his palazzo. A driver got out of the limo, opening the door for a well-dressed, dark-haired man, who went to talk to the security guard. Frowning, Alessandro sat up straight, narrowing his eyes, trying to see the man's face.

Then he did. And he rose to his feet with a half-strangled curse.

"Darling, what's wrong?" Olivia asked. "What is it?"

"Someone's here," he said curtly. "I have to go."

"Who could possibly pull you off the phone with me?"

"Théo St. Raphaël."

"What?" Olivia's voice was suddenly sharp. "You don't need to see him. Wait at your house, I'll pick you up and take you for lunch—"

"Sorry," he said shortly, and he hung up, tossing his phone on his desk. As he ran down the stairs, his blood was pounding for battle. His hands were clenched into fists, ready for a fight, any fight. Brushing past his bewildered housekeeper, he went into the courtyard.

"Let him in," Alessandro ordered his guard in Italian. Théo St. Raphaël came through the gate, looking polished and powerful in a suit and yellow tie, holding a leather briefcase. He looked calm, cool and under control, all things Alessandro hadn't felt for a week. The hot Italian sun shone down on his scrubby T-shirt and jeans as Alessandro stalked through the dusty courtyard to finally meet his rival.

"What the hell do you want?" he demanded. "Come to gloat?"

Théo St. Raphaël stared at him as if he were insane. "Gloat?"

"I bet you and—" he still couldn't say her name out loud "—your cousin had a good laugh after she helped you steal the Mexico City deal. It was clever for her to lure me into giving information in bed!"

In a swift movement, St. Raphaël leapt five steps across the courtyard in a flutter of dust and punched Alessandro solidly across the jaw.

"That's for Lilley," he said, panting as he rubbed his wrist. "Damn you."

It would have knocked a lesser man to the ground. As it was, Alessandro felt the impact of the blow all the way to his knees.

His own fist flew back on instinct. Then he straightened, rubbing his jaw. "At least you have the decency to attack me to my face, St. Raphaël," he said. "Rather than stabbing me in the back."

"Lilley kept one small secret from you. *One.*"

"Small?" Alessandro said incredulously. "She told you my plans for the Mexico City deal! Convinced me to marry her when she was in love with another man! And worst of all…" He cut himself off, and his voice hardened. "Why are you here? What more could she possibly want?"

The Frenchman glared at him. "In your office."

Alessandro stiffened, then realized his security guard was watching with interest, as were the paparazzi who'd been parked across the street ever since the scandalous night of their reception. He set his jaw. "Fine."

Turning on his heel, he led the count silently into the palazzo.

"I'm here to collect Lilley's things," St. Raphaël informed him once they reached his study. "Her tools. Her mother's quilt."

"And the clothes I bought her?"

"She doesn't want them."

Alessandro sank into his office chair, feeling weary. He swiveled towards the window. He'd nearly thrown her most precious belongings away in his rage after she'd disappeared, but he hadn't been able to do it. The tools and quilt were too much a part of what he'd loved about her. "It's boxed up by the front door. Help yourself." He glared at the other man. "I'll be glad to get it all out of here."

St. Raphaël stared at him coldly, then set his briefcase

on the desk. Opening it, he pulled out a file and held it to Alessandro.

"What's this?" he asked, not touching it.

"The Mexico City deal," St. Raphaël said scornfully. "If you still want it."

Alessandro opened the file. Skimming through it, he realized it was a contract to exchange Joyería for the St. Raphaël vineyard. He looked for a catch. He couldn't find one.

"I will step away from the Tokyo deal as well."

Alessandro looked up in bewilderment. "I don't understand."

"Lilley's idea."

"But why would she arrange this, when she's the one who betrayed me?"

"Lilley didn't betray you," St. Raphaël bit out. "Someone else gave me that information. She said she wanted payback for the way you replaced her with some cheap file-room girl." He paused. "I had no idea she was talking about Lilley."

"Olivia?" Alessandro said in a strangled voice. "Olivia Bianchi?"

St. Raphaël's eyes settled on his. "The two of you deserve each other."

Was it possible he was telling the truth? Had Olivia betrayed him? Alessandro suddenly remembered all the times he'd done business on the phone in the back of the limo, with Olivia sitting bored beside him. She'd certainly known about his rivalry with St. Raphaël.

She'd had motive, means and opportunity.

The Frenchman leaned forward, his knuckles white against the desk. "But you must promise, in writing, that you will keep the design studio in Mexico City. I gave

Rodriguez my word that none of his people would lose their jobs. And, unlike you, I do not wish to be a liar."

Alessandro's eyes narrowed. "I didn't lie. I might have *implied—*"

"You lied. Worse than Lilley ever did. All she was trying to do was get a job. You were trying to enrich your own pockets at the expense of someone else's honor. You lied to Rodriguez. Just as you lied to Lilley when you didn't mention until after you were wed that you wouldn't allow her to work."

Alessandro's cheeks grew hot. Then his chin lifted coldly. "Lilley slept with another man, then tried to pass off her unborn child as mine."

With a snort, St. Raphaël stared at him, then shook his head. "If you believe that, you're even more stupid than I thought." He pulled out one last paper. "Here. Give that to your lawyers."

I slept with a different man, just like you said. Alessandro remembered Lilley's wide, stricken eyes as she stood in her pink ballgown amid the holly and ivy. He remembered the strange way her voice had trembled. *And I loved him.*

Alessandro's heart gave a sickening lurch.

What if Alessandro was the man she'd loved—before he'd turned on her so brutally, in public, with his ex-mistress egging him on, practically chortling with glee?

He'd vowed to honor and protect his wife. Why hadn't he cared for her enough to speak with her privately? To ask, to listen, to give her the chance to explain? Instead, he'd turned on her like a rabid dog. He'd attacked her, his beautiful wife who had never done anything but love him with all of her gentle, loyal heart.

"Where is she?" he whispered.

"She left France a few hours ago." The other man's lips

pressed together in a thin line. "She wanted to visit her father, then scout out locations for her jewelry line."

"She's doing it?" Alessandro said faintly. "Really doing it?"

St. Raphaël glared at him. "My wife says Lilley's jewelry is a sure thing. And she should know." He drummed his fingers on the desk. "You know, I should thank you. For doing the right thing by my cousin."

Alessandro's lips lifted humorlessly. "You mean marrying her?"

"Divorcing her," he replied coldly. "Lilley is the kindest person I know. She doesn't have a mean bone in her body. She and her baby deserve better than you." He closed his briefcase with a snap. "But business is business. I have wanted these vineyards back for some time. Have your lawyers review the documents. There is no need for us to meet again. *Adieu.*"

Without another word, Théo St. Raphaël left. Numbly, Alessandro stared down at the file, and at the divorce papers still spread across his desk beneath. Picking up a page, he tried to read it, but the words seemed to move and jump across the pages. It was as if he were suddenly seeing the world from Lilley's point of view.

Pushing the papers aside, he rose to his feet. From the window, he saw St. Raphaël carry a large box out through the gate. His limousine soon disappeared back into the streets of Rome.

Alessandro looked up. The bright-blue sky seemed smeared violet. As if the world were going dark.

I love you, Alessandro.

I'm yours. Forever.

He closed his eyes, pressing his hot forehead against the cold glass of the window. But even with his eyes closed, even if he covered his ears with his hands, he could still hear Lilley's shaking voice, still see the grief in her eyes. *I'm done trying to make you love me. Done.*

And the truth hit Alessandro like a blow.

Lilley hadn't betrayed him.

He had betrayed her.

His eyes flew open. He'd told her she wasn't good enough to be his wife, or good enough to be liked by his friends. He'd insisted on buying her clothes. He'd told her why her jewelry would never sell, then insisted that she give up her own dreams in order to sit alone in their palazzo, waiting for him to come home.

He'd let her love him without offering her anything in return, except coldly expensive jewels, which he should have realized long ago, she would never, ever want.

No wonder when he'd turned on her so viciously at their reception, Lilley had finally given up. For months, she'd bent over backwards trying to please him. She'd convinced herself he was worthy of her love. That night, even her romantic, loyal heart had been forced to see the truth.

He'd finally proven that he wasn't her knight in shining armor, and never could be.

She was right. He'd been afraid to love her, terrified to let himself be vulnerable again. For sixteen years, he'd kept his heart locked up. When Olivia had given him an escape, his cowardly heart had taken the first chance at the exit door.

Lilley was right. Cold rage filled him. Rage at himself.

Alessandro turned back to the window, staring at the early twilight of December. The blue sky was streaked with pink and orange, like a brilliant fire on the horizon.

We all must choose in this life, he'd told her once. *The safety of a prison. Or the terrible joy that comes with freedom.*

He'd thought of her as a timid little mouse. But all along,

she was the one with the courageous heart. He was the one who'd been hiding.

But not anymore. *Not anymore.*

Whirling around, he grabbed the phone off his desk so fast he nearly it knocked to the floor.

He would bring the laughter and trust back to her eyes, even if it made him look like the biggest fool on the face of the earth. If he couldn't even do that…then that bastard St. Raphaël was right. Lilley and his child really would be better off without him.

Alessandro would find her. Win her.

Squaring his shoulders, he set his jaw.

He would deserve her.

After six hours, Lilley's backside was well and truly sore.

She shifted on the hard cushion of her father's reproduction Louis XIV couch as she sat in his fancy parlor. She looked down at her watch. Six hours he'd made her wait now. *Six.* It was her first visit in three years, and he'd just left her here, alone and unwelcome in the sprawling house he'd built for his mistress, a forty-thousand-square-foot mansion on a sprawling estate near Minneapolis.

Clearly this was her punishment for not coming home in June to marry his employee, as he'd demanded.

Her lower back gave a sudden stab of pain, and she rose to her feet. The parlor had beautiful views of snowy Lake Minnetonka through the black, bare trees, but it still felt like an office, not a home. There were no personal photographs, just posters from various Hainsbury's advertising campaigns. The closest framed poster showed a happy young couple embracing on a park bench with the image of an engagement ring superimposed around them. Beneath it in big letters was the tagline, Hainsbury Jewelers. When Only Perfection Will Do.

Perfection. Engagement rings. Love in general. Lilley hated them all right now. But most of all, she hated her knack for loving men who did not have the capacity or desire to love her back.

Her father's abandonment had left a hole in her heart. But Alessandro had done far worse. He'd cut through that hole with a machete, leaving one side of her heart drenched in acid, the other smashed with a meat mallet.

She'd given her husband everything, and it still hadn't been enough. Alessandro hadn't even tried to hear her side. He'd just taken Olivia's every word as gospel—even believing it was possible Lilley might have slept with another man!

Well, she *had* slept with another man. Without thinking, she reached up and touched the brass-and-pink-rock-crystal necklace hanging around her throat, a gesture she'd repeated many times over the last week. A tragedy that the man she'd loved, the man she'd been so sure Alessandro could be, had been entirely a figment of her imagination.

She swallowed, blinking fast. But work would see her through. After all she'd endured, she was no longer afraid of failure.

She just hadn't been thinking big enough. Instead of opening a boutique, she was starting her own line of handmade, unique jewelry art, as Vladimir Xendzov had called it. After Alessandro had effectively ended their marriage, Lilley had spent days weeping in her old housekeeper's suite in her cousin's castle before she'd resurfaced to play with her cousin's baby. Théo's wife had demanded, "Where did you get that fabulous necklace?"

"I made it myself," Lilley had replied, turning away. Then something inside her made her pause. Made her turn back around. With a deep breath, she'd added, "I've decided to start my own business. I'm going to sell handcrafted jewelry to luxury boutiques and exclusive department stores across the world. I'm going back to the States to try for a business loan."

Carrie had shaken her head vehemently. "No!" she'd cried, and for a moment Lilley was taken aback. Then her friend smiled. "Don't take out a loan with some banker, please. Let me do it! This is just the investment I was looking for."

Closing her eyes, Lilley took a deep breath. Her dream was coming true in a way she'd never imagined. She had her financing now and was dependent on no one, not even Carrie. She'd finally been brave enough to take a risk. Alessandro had helped her do that, she admitted quietly to herself. He'd taught her how to have the confidence to follow her dreams. Her business might succeed or fail, but either way, it was all up to her.

She'd finally become strong enough to stand up for what was right, even if it terrified her. And she would rather be alone than be with a husband who didn't love or trust her.

Lilley was no man's housekeeper. No man's helpless wife. And apparently, no man's daughter.

As the sun started to set, scattering pink light over the snow beneath a black lattice of trees, Lilley finally gave up and turned for the door.

"What do you want?" Her father's voice was low and hard. Lilley saw him in the doorway, and her mouth fell open with shock.

Walton Hainsbury seemed to have aged decades in the three years since her mother's funeral. His beady eyes glared at her through his wire-rimmed glasses, but his face looked pale as he took a long suck of his cigar.

Her nose wrinkled at the smell. Cigars had become her least favorite smell in the world. He'd been smoking the day he'd left Lilley and her mother, when he'd announced he would go and build a mansion on Lake Minnetonka for his far younger mistress. Eighteen-year-old Lilley had cared for her mother at their family home in Minneapolis for two years, until she died.

"What are you doing here?" Walton rasped, looking contemptuously at the powder-blue coat and dark, fitted jeans. "Have you come crawling here to try to worm your way back into my will? It's too late, missy! I've left everything to charity!"

Lilley stiffened. "I didn't come for money."

"Likely story."

The accusation stung. "I've never asked you for money. Not once. You know I haven't." Lifting her chin, she looked at him. "I just came to tell you you're going to be a grandfather."

He stared at her. She noticed that the color of his skin was ashy, his jowls flabby, as if he'd lost weight. He took several puffs of his cigar before he said in a low voice, "You're pregnant?"

She nodded.

His eyes narrowed at her bare left hand. "And no husband." He glared at her. "You couldn't marry the man I chose for you. Had to throw yourself away!"

"The man you chose for me was twice my age."

"If you'd married him, I could have left him my company. I would have known you'd always have someone to take care of you. But you wouldn't see sense, as usual. And now it's too late."

She heard a wistfulness in his voice. A lump rose in her throat. "I'll be all right. I can take care of myself."

"You can't," he barked. "You've just come back with another mouth to feed, expecting me to solve things for you as I always do."

The accusation was so unjust, she sucked in her breath.

"You've never solved anything for me! You just made me feel helpless and stupid as a kid. The instant you knew about my dyslexia, you treated me differently. Same as you did when Mom got sick!"

"I loved your mother," he said harshly. "As I loved you. I tried to take care of you both—"

"By divorcing her when she was dying? By deserting us both so you could build—" She looked around the gilded parlor. "—*this* for your mistress? Where is Tiffany, by the way?"

Walton looked away. "She left me a few months ago."

"Oh." Lilley blinked at him, not knowing what to say. *Good riddance* seemed rude.

"I never wanted to leave your mother," he added gruffly. "Paula's the one who told me to go."

Lilley's brow furrowed. "What?"

He exhaled. "I've never dealt well with illness, I'll give you that. But when I told your mother about Tiffany, I was trying to wipe the slate clean. I vowed to her that if she could forgive me, I'd be a better husband, a better man." His lips trembled in a smile. "But she told me to get the hell out of our house. She refused to see me again. And so I didn't." He clawed back his wispy hair. "Not until the funeral, when she couldn't stop me."

"I never knew. I just assumed—"

"Your mother didn't want to drag you into our quarrel. I respected her wishes."

"And took all the blame," she whispered.

He looked at her. "I reckon I deserved it." He looked away. "So who's your baby's father? Some penniless musician? An artist? Any chance the man has a shred of honor or decency?"

"If you're asking if he's married me, the answer is yes. We were married in September in Las Vegas."

His face grew more ashen. His long eyebrows shook as he said, "You got married! Without telling me!"

"You disinherited me. I didn't think you'd care."

"Tell me you got a prenup."

"No."

His hand trembled as he stabbed the cigar towards her. "I haven't worked hard all my life to let some greedy fortune hunter steal it all now!"

"He doesn't want your money," she whispered. She looked away. "And anyway, he's about to divorce me."

"After such a short marriage? Who will take care of you and the child?"

"I will." She took a shallow breath, trying not to inhale his smoke which was making her feel sick. "Théo offered me a spot at his headquarters in Paris, in his mergers and acquisitions department. He said I have a fresh take on things, an original mind. But his wife Carrie and I had already decided—"

"Original mind?" her father interrupted derisively. "You can't survive on your own, and take care of my grandchild alone. You will come home," he ordered. "You'll move in with me."

Lilley sucked in her breath. "Why can't you believe in me, Dad? Just once?" she whispered. "Why can't you forget my dyslexia and tell me you believe in me, tell me I can do anything I put my mind to?"

Walton scowled. "Lilley—"

"Forget it." She turned away. "Good-bye."

Leaving the parlor, she fled the mansion. Outside, the frigid Minnesota air hit her skin with a vengeance, making her shiver in her warm jacket. Cold December light gleamed off Lake Minnetonka, and she could see a white cloud of fog rising up from the ice as she climbed back into her rental car. Starting the engine, she drove down the gravel driveway, her back tires sliding over the packed snow.

But when she reached the gate, the security guard ignored her. She waved at him furiously, but he turned the other way, a phone to his ear. Finally, she got out of the car and stomped to the guardhouse. "Open it," she demanded. "Right now!"

The guard pushed the button to open the gate, but leaned out of his window. "Mr. Hainsbury wants you to wait."

Lilley muttered under her breath. She was done waiting for anyone, especially men who'd proven over and over in every possible way that they didn't love her. Climbing into her car, she gunned the engine. "Let him wait."

But as she pulled out of the long driveway and out onto the quiet country road, she saw her father run through the gate, waving his arms as he shouted after her. For a moment, she stared towards the inviting open road. Then, cursing herself aloud, she slammed on the brake.

Lilley closed her eyes, heart pounding as she leaned her head against the steering wheel. Then, slowly, she turned off the engine.

She climbed out of the car, turning back towards her father. He was wheezing loudly and his run slowed to a walk. But she didn't take a single step. She let him walk all the way.

"You don't know, do you?" he said in a low voice. "Before I found out about the baby, I thought that was the only reason you turned up here. Because you found out."

"Found out what?"

He looked at her. "I'm dying, Lilley."

She stared at him, not moving. "What?"

He gave her a wan smile. "That's why Tiffany left." He held up the lit cigar between his fingers and stared down at it. "Doctors give me a few months, maybe a year. I wanted you to marry Gerald because…then I'd have known," he whispered. "That you'd always be all right."

Trembling, Lilley looked at her father in the gray December light. She'd had a happy childhood, back when her parents had loved each other. Her father had taught her to ride a bike. Taught her how to weld. He'd taught her how to evaluate uncut gems, and the different names for the stones. He'd shown her, through his example, the value of hard work and big dreams. She exhaled.

"There's no hope?"

He dropped the cigar, crushing it beneath his feet. "Nope." His lips creased. "I've made a lot of mistakes, Lilley. First with your mother—then with you. But even I couldn't be stupid enough to make this last one, and let you leave, knowing I might never see you again." He lifted his head. "I do love you, Lilley," he whispered. "And I've always been proud of you. I know I wasn't always a good father, and I'm sorry. But before I die, I need…I'm asking—" His voice cracked. "—for you to forgive me."

Lilley stared at him, her heart squeezing in her chest. Even her mother had forgiven Walton at the last. He'd treated them both badly. But she suddenly knew she wasn't going to let him die alone.

Narrowing her eyes, she shook her head decisively. "Not going to happen."

Her father's face fell. Then she added with an unsteady smile, "There's no way you're going to die. I know you, Dad. Death itself wouldn't be able to talk you into a deal you didn't like."

He exhaled. He looked up, and his eyes were filled with tears. "I told you that you needed me. That was a lie. The truth is—I'm the one who needs you." He swallowed. "I swear to you, if I live long enough, I'll be a better grandfather than I was a father."

She felt a lump in her throat. "You weren't so bad. Really."

"No?"

"Well." She gave him a crooked smile. "You did teach me how to ride a bike." He smiled back at her. But as she started to reach out to him, the road suddenly rumbled and shook beneath her feet. She heard a loud honking behind her.

Turning in surprise, she saw a delivery van barreling down the country road, followed by a semitruck so huge it hung over the edges of the asphalt. The delivery van drove by, honking.

"What the devil?" her father sputtered, coughing.

"Abbott," she whispered in shock. What was Alessandro's chauffeur doing in Minnesota, driving a delivery van on this small country road?

The semi parked behind her car, blocking her on one side as the delivery van blocked the other. Confused, she started walking towards Abbott, who'd leapt out of the driver's seat and was swiftly walking around to the back of the van.

"Abbott, what are you doing here?"

She stopped as he opened the van's back doors. Looking inside, Lilley sucked in her breath, her hand over her mouth.

There was a knight in the back of the van. A medieval knight in full armor.

The knight pushed up his visor, and she saw Alessandro's dark, handsome face. His warm black eyes were glowing with such adoration that her heart caught in her throat.

She exhaled, tilting her head to look up at him in the back of the van. She'd slipped on the ice and fallen into some kind of coma. She was dreaming. That was the only explanation for Alessandro wearing armor in Minnesota, standing in the back of a van, in front of a snowy white lake.

"What are you doing here?" she breathed.

"I've come for you," Alessandro said, his eyes looking straight into hers. "I was a coward and a fool. Come back to me, Lilley," he whispered. "Let me show you I can be the husband you always dreamed of."

Tears filled her eyes as she went towards the van. With a scrape of metal, he hopped off the van's edge. But the heavy weight of his armor seemed to take him off guard. His visor snapped shut with a loud clang as he fell heavily on the snowy road.

Lilley was beside him in an instant, kneeling as she gathered him in her arms. "Are you all right?" she said anxiously. "Are you hurt?"

Sprawled out across the road, Alessandro didn't move. Dear God, what if a sharp blow in that tin-can suit had knocked him out? Lilley's hands shook as she pulled up his visor.

But she saw he was silently laughing. She fell back on her haunches in wonder.

"Oh my God. You've totally made a fool of yourself," she breathed in awe. She shook her head, suddenly smiling. "Dressing up in armor? What were you thinking?"

"I've never seen any angel half as beautiful as you." He lifted his armored hand to touch her cheek. "I would battle far more than armor to be in the arms of the woman I love. I would slay dragons for you," he whispered.

What had he said? *What had he just said?* That he loved her? She felt her heart expand and bend and swell until it was big enough to swallow the whole world. She looked down, her lashes brushing shyly against her cheek. "Come on," she murmured. "I'll help you up."

But the armor was even heavier than she'd thought. First Abbott, then her father, had to come and help him to stand up.

"Hello, sir," Alessandro said to her father, smiling.

"I don't think we've ever met in person. I'm Alessandro Caetani."

Walton blinked, his eyes wide. He looked at Lilley. "This is your husband?" he asked faintly.

Unable to speak, she nodded, then turned back to Alessandro.

Behind her, she heard her father give a low whistle. "What a merger this will make." But as she turned with a scowl, Walton quickly said to Abbott, "Care for a drink at the gatehouse? Something to warm your blood?"

"You bet."

Lilley and Alessandro stood alone on the snowy, empty road. A wind blew off the lake, whipping through her hair, but she no longer felt the cold. She felt warm all over, filled with light.

"What possessed you to do this?" she whispered, putting her hand on the side of his shiny helmet. "This crazy thing?"

He moved his metal glove over her hand. "I wanted to show you I'm sorry," he said in a low voice. "I never should have asked if the baby was mine."

She swallowed, looking down.

"I shouldn't have let a single white lie keep me from trusting you for thousands of reasons," he said. "One most of all." He lifted her chin with his finger. "I love you, Lilley."

The winter sun burst through the gray winter clouds. A beam of light caught his armor, making him sparkle like diamonds.

"It took losing you in Rome to make me realize you were right. I was afraid. Now, the only thing that scares me is losing you. I'll do anything to win you back, Lilley," he whispered. His dark eyes met hers. "Absolutely anything."

The white, gray and black of winter suddenly filled with

the beautiful pinks and greens of spring in Lilley's eyes. He loved her. And their lives together were only beginning.

"I love you, Alessandro," she whispered, throwing her arms around his hard, cold armor.

For a long moment, they held each other on the quiet road. Then Lilley pulled back, her forehead furrowed as she glanced back at the huge semitruck, still parked behind her car. "But why did you bring that?"

"Oh." Alessandro gave her a sudden grin. "I was afraid I'd kill us both if I actually tried to sit on a horse, so I made other plans." Looking at the truck's driver, he motioned with his hand. The driver hopped out and went to the back of the truck. She heard the distant roar of an engine, and then a vintage Cadillac De Ville—in hot pink—rolled off the ramp to park beside them.

As the driver disappeared for his drink at the gatehouse, Lilley walked slowly around the Cadillac, her mouth open.

It was a classic convertible from the 1960s, the exact same fuchsia as the ball gown she'd worn to their reception in Rome. "What is that?"

He grinned at her. "Our getaway vehicle, *cara.* To ride off into the sunset."

She looked back at him. "And what if you hadn't found me? What if I'd already been gone?"

"Then I would have sold my business and driven all over the country, looking for you," he said gravely behind her. "Everywhere. Until you were in my arms."

She gasped a laugh. "Dressed as a knight? Driving a hot-pink Cadillac? The paparazzi would have had a field day! They'd have said you'd lost your mind!"

"I have," he said softly. "Along with my heart. All I want to do, for the rest of my life, is make a fool of myself. Over you."

Tears fell from Lilley's lashes. Standing on her tiptoes,

she held up his cold visor with her fingertips and kissed him. Her husband kissed her back fervently, reverently, passionately. They had been standing in the snowy road for hours, or perhaps minutes, when she finally pulled away for air. His black eyes glimmered down at her. She had no idea if the tears on his cheeks were hers or his. But what did it matter? They were one.

"Thank you for being a fool," she said, her heart welling with joy. "Thank you for making all my childhood dreams come true."

He looked down at her, his handsome face glowing with love and shining with the strength of steel. "And thank you," he whispered, stroking her cheek, "for making me want to dance."

They danced at their first anniversary party the following September. As Alessandro led Lilley to the dance floor in their Sonoma ballroom, he whirled her in a circle, making her colorful skirts twirl. She heard a soft *"awww"* from their fifty or so guests, just family and friends, including a deep sigh from her father, who was holding his baby grandson, Teo.

Alessandro pulled her close on the dance floor. Lilley looked up at him breathlessly as he swayed against her.

"My, oh my," she murmured, fluttering her eyelashes. "You're quite the dancer. Have you been taking lessons?"

"You know I have. You've been taking them with me." He twirled her, then gave a mischievous grin. "No broken toes in sight."

"Because you're leading me."

"No," he whispered, pulling her close. "We lead each other."

Lilley looked up at him, dazed with happiness. Their lives over the past ten months had been filled with one joy after the next. They now split their time evenly between Rome and San Francisco, where Lilley had started her fledgling jewelry company, Lilley Caetani Limited. Her first collection had already been a great success at the international jewelry trade show in San Francisco.

So much had changed in the last year. Lilley was still awed to think how, just fifteen months before, she'd attended the trade show as a guest with a dream. Now she was an exhibitor. With Carrie's financial backing, her fledgling company had already made a splash in the trade dailies and orders had started to flood in from around the world. She would have to hire more employees soon. Lilley often traveled with her husband and their baby to Singapore or Norway or Namibia, getting inspiration for her designs. She happily traveled wherever the continuing expansion of Caetani Worldwide took them.

There was only one of Alessandro's potential acquisitions that she absolutely wouldn't allow. Alessandro had made multiple offers to buy her company and merge it with Caetani-Hainsbury Worldwide, which she'd refused in no uncertain terms.

"Sorry, my company is not for sale," she'd said breezily. "I'm not interested in being part of some soulless, heartless conglomerate—"

"Hey!"

She'd grinned. "Sorry. But my company is small and I like it that way."

He'd tilted his head thoughtfully. "We could double your growth projections, especially in Europe. And there might be other fringe benefits as well," he'd murmured. "Think about it."

"Not for sale at any price," she said primly.

He'd lifted a wicked eyebrow. "Oh? Are you sure?" And he'd pulled her into bed. Lilley sighed at the memory. Of course, she would never sell him her company, but it was sure fun to let him try.

Tonight's anniversary party in Sonoma had been Alessandro's idea. He'd planned the whole thing from start to finish. The wine harvest looked to be excellent this year, and all their friends and family beamed as they held up glasses, toasting Alessandro and Lilley on the occasion of their one-year anniversary.

Olivia Bianchi, alas, was not in attendance. Lilley hadn't even tried to invite her. She'd learned she couldn't please everyone, and she didn't need to impress anyone. The only people she cared about were right here: her friends Nadia and Jeremy, who were now engaged. And her family. Her cousin had come all the way from France, along with Carrie and their baby. Alessandro and Théo might never be friends, but they'd managed to achieve a sort of détente. They'd moved their rivalry to the realms of basketball and extreme sports like skydiving. Great, Lilley thought with an inward groan. Just what she needed. A husband and a cousin who were fighting to jump out of a perfectly good plane.

Even her father was doing better, now that he'd retired and given up day-to-day management of Hainsbury's to Alessandro. The company was on track to merge with Caetani Worldwide, and all of it would be left in trust to Walton's grandchildren. Her father had moved to San Francisco to be closer to them, and to focus on getting healthier. And, like a miracle, he seemed stronger every day. Especially on the days he played with his grandson.

Friends and family were all that mattered, Lilley thought. Not fame. Not the glitter of wealth. The only diamonds that mattered were the ones in the bright smiles of the people she loved. As her dance with Alessandro ended and their friends applauded wildly around them, her father brought the baby to the dance floor.

"I think the kid wants to dance," Walton said gruffly.

A new song began, and Alessandro took baby Teo in his arms. Nuzzling his chubby cheeks and downy head, he looked down at his son tenderly. "I can teach him."

Lilley's heart swelled as Alessandro held their cooing baby against his tuxedo jacket, and wrapped his other arm around her. Smiling, she leaned her head against her husband's strong shoulders as they swayed together in time to the music. Listening to Teo's baby giggle and Alessandro's joyful baritone laugh, Lilley suddenly knew their lives together would always be happy like this. Their days would shine with endless brilliant facets, in a hodgepodge of sparkling gemstones and tarnished brass, rough rock crystals and gleaming platinum, that when welded together…formed a family.

* * * * *

Mills & Boon® Hardback

February 2012

ROMANCE

An Offer She Can't Refuse	Emma Darcy
An Indecent Proposition	Carol Marinelli
A Night of Living Dangerously	Jennie Lucas
A Devilishly Dark Deal	Maggie Cox
Marriage Behind the Façade	Lynn Raye Harris
Forbidden to His Touch	Natasha Tate
Back in the Lion's Den	Elizabeth Power
Running From the Storm	Lee Wilkinson
Innocent 'til Proven Otherwise	Amy Andrews
Dancing with Danger	Fiona Harper
The Cop, the Puppy and Me	Cara Colter
Back in the Soldier's Arms	Soraya Lane
Invitation to the Prince's Palace	Jennie Adams
Miss Prim and the Billionaire	Lucy Gordon
The Shameless Life of Ruiz Acosta	Susan Stephens
Who Wants To Marry a Millionaire?	Nicola Marsh
Sydney Harbour Hospital: Lily's Scandal	Marion Lennox
Sydney Harbour Hospital: Zoe's Baby	Alison Roberts

HISTORICAL

The Scandalous Lord Lanchester	Anne Herries
His Compromised Countess	Deborah Hale
Destitute On His Doorstep	Helen Dickson
The Dragon and the Pearl	Jeannie Lin

MEDICAL

Gina's Little Secret	Jennifer Taylor
Taming the Lone Doc's Heart	Lucy Clark
The Runaway Nurse	Dianne Drake
The Baby Who Saved Dr Cynical	Connie Cox

ROMANCE

The Most Coveted Prize	Penny Jordan
The Costarella Conquest	Emma Darcy
The Night that Changed Everything	Anne McAllister
Craving the Forbidden	India Grey
Her Italian Soldier	Rebecca Winters
The Lonesome Rancher	Patricia Thayer
Nikki and the Lone Wolf	Marion Lennox
Mardie and the City Surgeon	Marion Lennox

HISTORICAL

Married to a Stranger	Louise Allen
A Dark and Brooding Gentleman	Margaret McPhee
Seducing Miss Lockwood	Helen Dickson
The Highlander's Return	Marguerite Kaye

MEDICAL

The Doctor's Reason to Stay	Dianne Drake
Career Girl in the Country	Fiona Lowe
Wedding on the Baby Ward	Lucy Clark
Special Care Baby Miracle	Lucy Clark
The Tortured Rebel	Alison Roberts
Dating Dr Delicious	Laura Iding

Mills & Boon® Hardback

March 2012

ROMANCE

Roccanti's Marriage Revenge	Lynne Graham
The Devil and Miss Jones	Kate Walker
Sheikh Without a Heart	Sandra Marton
Savas's Wildcat	Anne McAllister
The Argentinian's Solace	Susan Stephens
A Wicked Persuasion	Catherine George
Girl on a Diamond Pedestal	Maisey Yates
The Theotokis Inheritance	Susanne James
The Good, the Bad and the Wild	Heidi Rice
The Ex Who Hired Her	Kate Hardy
A Bride for the Island Prince	Rebecca Winters
Pregnant with the Prince's Child	Raye Morgan
The Nanny and the Boss's Twins	Barbara McMahon
Once a Cowboy...	Patricia Thayer
Mr Right at the Wrong Time	Nikki Logan
When Chocolate Is Not Enough...	Nina Harrington
Sydney Harbour Hospital: Luca's Bad Girl	Amy Andrews
Falling for the Sheikh She Shouldn't	Fiona McArthur

HISTORICAL

Untamed Rogue, Scandalous Mistress	Bronwyn Scott
Honourable Doctor, Improper Arrangement	Mary Nichols
The Earl Plays With Fire	Isabelle Goddard
His Border Bride	Blythe Gifford

MEDICAL

Dr Cinderella's Midnight Fling	Kate Hardy
Brought Together by Baby	Margaret McDonagh
The Firebrand Who Unlocked His Heart	Anne Fraser
One Month to Become a Mum	Louisa George

Mills & Boon® Large Print

March 2012

ROMANCE

The Power of Vasilii	Penny Jordan
The Real Rio D'Aquila	Sandra Marton
A Shameful Consequence	Carol Marinelli
A Dangerous Infatuation	Chantelle Shaw
How a Cowboy Stole Her Heart	Donna Alward
Tall, Dark, Texas Ranger	Patricia Thayer
The Boy is Back in Town	Nina Harrington
Just An Ordinary Girl?	Jackie Braun

HISTORICAL

The Lady Gambles	Carole Mortimer
Lady Rosabella's Ruse	Ann Lethbridge
The Viscount's Scandalous Return	Anne Ashley
The Viking's Touch	Joanna Fulford

MEDICAL

Cort Mason – Dr Delectable	Carol Marinelli
Survival Guide to Dating Your Boss	Fiona McArthur
Return of the Maverick	Sue MacKay
It Started with a Pregnancy	Scarlet Wilson
Italian Doctor, No Strings Attached	Kate Hardy
Miracle Times Two	Josie Metcalfe